HONEY MOON

A SCARY LITTLE CHRISTMAS

by

Sofi Benitez

with Joyce Magnin

Illustrations by Christina Weidman

Created by Mark Andrew Poe

rabbit publishers

A Scary Little Christmas (Honey Moon)
By Sofi Benitez
with Joyce Magnin
Created by Mark Andrew Poe

Rabbit Publishers
1624 W. Northwest Highway
Arlington Heights, IL 60004

Illustrations by Christina Weidman
Cover design by Megan Black
Interior Design by Lewis Design & Marketing

ISBN: 978-1-943785-69-8

10 9 8 7 6 5 4 3 2 1

1. Fiction - Action and Adventure 2. Children's Fiction
First Color Edition
Printed in U.S.A.

I go where I am needed.

— Honey Moon

TABLE OF CONTENTS

PREFACE

Halloween visited the little town of Sleepy Hollow and never left. Many moons ago, a sly and evil mayor found the powers of darkness helpful in building Sleepy Hollow into "Spooky Town," one of the country's most celebrated attractions. Now, years later, the indomitable Honey Moon is choosing to make life difficult for the mayor and his evil associates.

Welcome to the enchanted world of Honey Moon. Halloween may have found a home in Sleepy Hollow, but Honey and her friends are going to make sure it doesn't get the best of them.

FAMILY

Honey Moon

Honey is ten years old. She is in the fifth grade at Sleepy Hollow Elementary School. She loves to read, and she loves to spend time with her friends. Honey is sassy and spirited and doesn't have any trouble speaking her mind—even if it gets her grounded once in a while. Honey has a strong sensor when it comes to knowing right from wrong and good from evil and, like she says, when it comes to doing the right thing— Honey goes where she is needed.

Harry Moon

Harry is Honey's older brother. He is thirteen years old and in the eighth grade at Sleepy Hollow Middle School. Harry is a magician. And not just a kid magician who does kid tricks, nope, Harry has the true gift of magic.

Harvest Moon

Harvest is the baby of the Moon family. He is two years old. Sometimes Honey has to watch him, but she mostly doesn't mind.

Mary Moon

Mary Moon is the mom. She is fair and straightforward with her kids. She loves them dearly, and they know it. Mary works full time as a nurse, so she often relies on her family for help around the house.

John Moon

John is the dad. He's a bit of a nerd. He works as an IT professional, and sometimes he thinks he would love it if his children followed in his footsteps. But he respects that Harry, Honey, and possibly Harvest will need to go their own way. John owns a classic sports car he calls Emma.

III

Half Moon

Half Moon is the family dog. He is big and clumsy and has floppy ears. Half is pretty much your basic dog.

FRIENDS

Becky Young

Becky is Honey's best friend. They've known each other since pre-school. Becky is quiet and smart. She is an artist. She is loyal to Honey and usually lets Honey take the lead, but occasionally, Becky makes her thoughts known. And she has really great ideas.

Claire Sinclair

Claire is also Honey's friend. She's a bit bossy, like Honey, so they sometimes clash. Claire is an athlete. She enjoys all sports but especially soccer, softball, and basketball. Sometimes kids poke fun at her rhyming name. But she doesn't mind—not one bit.

Brianna Royal

Brianna is also one of Honey's classmates. Brianna is different from all the other kids. She definitely dances to her own music. Brianna is very special. She seems to know things before they happen and always shows up in the nick of time when a friend is in trouble.

Isabela Bonito Stevens

Isabela is Honey's newest friend. Isabela volunteers at the Sleepy Hollow Animal Shelter. Animals are her thing, and she has never met a fur baby she didn't love. Honey is showing Isabela the ropes of living in Spooky Town.

FOES

Clarice Maxine Kligore

Clarice is Honey's arch nemesis. For some reason Clarice doesn't like Honey and tries to bully her. But Honey has no trouble standing up to her. The reason Clarice likes to hassle Honey probably has something to do with the fact that Honey knows the truth abut the Kligores. They are evil.

Maximus Kligore

The Honorable (or not-so-honorable depending on your viewpoint) Maximus Kligore is the mayor of Sleepy Hollow. He is the one who plunged Sleepy Hollow into a state of eternal Halloween. He said it was just a publicity stunt to raise town revenues and increase jobs. But Honey knows differently. She knows there is more to Kligore's plans—something so much more sinister.

THE VILE DELIVERY

oney Moon stood on the stage and slowly spun her shepherd's staff like a ninja ready to attack. The parts for the annual Christmas pageant had already been assigned, and changing Mrs. Keys's mind was harder than algebra. But that didn't keep Honey from trying.

"Sure, it'd be nice if Becky and I could both play the role of Mary," Honey said. "But since I've already memorized the lines, it only seems right that you switch the roles. Becky will do fine as a shepherd."

Her best friend Becky nodded in agreement. "Honey has never gotten to be Mary, and I was her last year. And she does have the lines memorized."

And that's why they were best friends— because Becky was a reasonable person, which was rare as far as ten-year-old girls went. Come to think of it, reasonable people were a rarity, no matter what their age.

Take Mrs. Keys for an example. How could she stick Honey in such an unimportant role? Shepherds were boring. The Moon family's fireplace manger scene had been missing one of the shepherds for quite a while and no one even cared or noticed. Which was good, because Honey distinctly remembered the Fourth of July when, thanks to a science experiment she was conducting, the shepherd rode the Dynamo

Exploding Patriotic Rocket bound for glory.

But if they lost the Mary figurine, the whole nativity set would have to be replaced. Which is exactly why Honey thought she should have the starring role. Someone with her natural charm, intellect, and skills should be wearing the pretty blue gown instead of the itchy shepherd robes.

"No," Mrs. Keys said to Becky. "You are perfect for Mary." Mrs. Keys had a big face, but she kept her eyes, nose, and mouth all crammed together in the center of it. "You have beautiful dark, curly hair—"

"Mary could have had brownish-blond hair, couldn't she?" Honey flipped a tangled ponytail over her shoulder. "Or I could wear a wig."

But Mrs. Keys shook her head. "Becky will play the part of Mary because Mary was gracious and kind and merciful. Mary did not argue or interrupt adults to tell them they were wrong and how to direct the pageant. Becky is nice, and for this role, a kind heart is more important than being a know-it-all."

4

Mrs. Keys's son, Scooter, who was tall, handsome, and in eighth grade, put his homework down, stood up in the front row, and clapped his hands. The smacks echoed loudly across the empty sanctuary. Honey lowered her shepherd's staff and glared at Scooter. They wouldn't treat her brother Harry with this kind of disrespect.

"Shepherds rule," Honey muttered even though she didn't quite mean it. She looked at Becky. "You'll have to memorize your lines from last year," she said. "I'll help you."

Becky smiled. "Thanks, Honey, and you'll be the best shepherd on stage."

Honey feigned her best smile and looked out over the sanctuary as the doors swung open and in walked a strange man. He was a tall, husky man in brown clothes carrying some kind of electronic gadget.

"Excuse me," the man called. "Am I in the right place?"

"Not unless you like bad singing and lame costumes," Scooter said.

Eighth graders didn't have to be in the play. That's why he could sit and make fun of them.

Mrs. Keys clomped off the stage in her heavy winter boots. "Can I help you, young man? We are in the middle of our Christmas rehearsal."

"Christmas rehearsal? Must be the right place." The delivery man punched some buttons on his electronic clipboard. "I'll be right back."

"I hope he has new, non-itchy shepherds' robes," Honey said.

"No new robes," Mrs. Keys said. "I can't imagine what he might have."

The delivery man pushed the sanctuary doors open and carried in a giant Santa Claus. "Had to take it out of the box," he said, "to fit through the door." But when he set it on its feet and turned it around, the kids all gasped. Santa had red, angry eyes. Vampire fangs stuck out of his beard, and his sack of toys had been replaced with a pitchfork held in blood-splattered gloves.

"Get that monster out of here!" Mrs. Keys said.

The delivery man scratched his head. "What do you want us to do with the rabid reindeer?"

The doors opened again, and a second delivery man walked in carrying a life-sized plastic reindeer that looked more like a werewolf than Rudolph. "This here is Slasher. Maggot, Cujo, and the rest are still in the truck."

Honey looked at her sock-covered feet. She had a low nightmare threshold. In plain words, that meant anything creepy, weird, or scary could give her nightmares worse than the elevator prank videos on YouTube. She had to look away. Pretend she was somewhere nice. Like her kitchen at home, feeding Jell-O to her little brother, Harvest.

Mrs. Keys did not yell. She said she never yelled. But she was using her lungs at one hundred percent, maybe one hundred and fifty percent. "Those do not belong here! Remove them at once!"

The first man looked at his electronic gadget. "Isn't this the place for the Haunted Holiday Festival?"

1

"I should say not!" Mrs. Keys said. "Those . . . those monstrosities belong outside, in the town green."

"Oh, gotcha," the delivery man said. "Where that big tent is."

Honey felt her brow wrinkle. She glanced at Becky who was looking a little confused also. "Haunted Holiday Festival?" Honey whispered.

Becky shrugged.

"Why?" Honey said. "Why do they have to make everything about Halloween? Even Christmas?"

"That's how Mayor Kligore wants it, I suppose," Becky said. "Nothing is safe when your town's motto is 'Where every day is Halloween night.'"

Honey's Christmas spirit drooped as she watched Mrs. Keys direct the delivery men to the town green. There wasn't anything she could do about it. This was Sleepy Hollow, Massachusetts where all the stores had creepy names like the

Witching Hour Candy Store and Screaming Jelly Bean, where even the streets were named for something scary, and where the local radio station played "Thriller," "Ghostbusters," and "Monster Mash" all year. But Honey didn't want a scary merry Christmas. No, Honey wanted a normal Christmas, not one with cobwebs and dripping fangs attached.

Finally, play practice ended. Honey was glad for that. First, she got picked over for the role of Mary, and now there was going to be a haunted celebration for all the world to see.

"It'll be okay," Becky said as they stood near the curb waiting for their moms. "You'll see."

I guess," Honey said. "I guess."

Mrs. Young, Becky's mom, pulled up to the curb.

"See you," Becky said.

Honey only nodded. She was kind of lost in thought. "There must be a way to keep scary Christmas from coming," she whispered.

GREAT EXPECTATIONS

The Moon Family minivan always smelled like french fries. Honey pulled the sliding door closed and buckled up.

"How was practice?" Mary Moon asked. "Did Becky remember her lines? There weren't any shepherds tripping over their robes this time, were there?" She looked in the rearview mirror. "No, no, Harvest. Only one fry. You have to share."

"I wish we could have a normal, traditional Christmas," Honey said. She plucked a fry from the small orange bag Harvest held. "A fun celebration with old-time music instead of all the weird Halloween stuff that goes on in this town. Whoever heard of a reindeer named Slasher?"

"What are you talking about?" her mother asked.

Honey caught her mother's eye in the rearview mirror. "Do you know what would be awesome?" Honey said. "What if our Christmas play was about the cosmic battle going on? What if angels had to protect the baby from these dark forces that were trying to hurt him? I bet it happened. And the angels wouldn't be in white robes but in armor. Shining armor. They'd be tough, and they wouldn't be afraid of any scary reindeer or vampire Santa Claus."

12

She'd said too much. Honey's mom fixed her with that I'm-about-to-learn-your-secrets-and-you-are-powerless-to-stop-me look. "What's this about a vampire Santa?"

They'd stopped at a stop sign near the town green. The big black tent sat like a huge menacing raven with its wings outstretched.

"Do you know about the Haunted Holiday Festival?" Honey asked.

"Yes, we're having it right there." Mary flipped her turn signal while nodding toward the field. "But I didn't know we were having a vampire Santa or a reindeer named Slasher."

"Slasher," Harvest said as he chewed on a fry.

"Well I saw him—fangs and all. And . . . and who's the 'we' you are talking about?"

"The town, I guess," Mary Moon said. "I haven't heard any names, come to think of it, and nothing about a planning committee."

13

And that was a bad sign.

Sleepy Hollow used to be just a regular town. Sure, with a name like Sleepy Hollow, people were always going to have their laughs. Honey Moon understood embarrassing names. But over the last few years, the town had changed. Mayor Kligore and the selectmen decided to make money on their famous name. Instead of telling visitors the truth—that the Sleepy Hollow they were looking for was in New York—and sending them on their way, they decided to become the spooky town from Washington Irving's famous story. And it worked. Tourists flocked to town, making money for everyone. Soon storefronts were filled with eerie displays. Fake cobwebs hung from every ceiling. Skeletons and bubbling cauldrons were everywhere. Almost no public place was safe from the dark decorations.

The main attraction was the horrifying bronze statue of the famous Headless Horseman that crackled with evil. It stood right smack-dab in the center of the town green, like Mr. Headless was a war hero or something. People flocked to it to take family pictures and selfies, but Honey just shook her head in disgust every time she passed it.

"They are going to decorate the tent with scary Christmas decorations," Honey said. "They even have rabid reindeer." She shuddered.

"The tourists will love it, but I have to agree with you on this one." Mary tapped the steering wheel. "Why can't Mayor Kligore just let Christmas be about good, not darkness? When I was a girl, I loved the pretty lights of Christmas. I especially loved the bells in the church steeple. They'd ring and ring, for hours it seemed."

"Bells? What bells?" Honey asked.

"The church bells, of course," said her mom as she turned the wheel and headed toward Shopper's Row. "They were amazing! Just think, Honey. High up in the church belfry were twelve bells, some bigger than the others to make different notes, but they were all cast in bronze and positively gorgeous in their ages-old patina. Twelve people would stand under them and pull the ropes that were attached to the wheels that turned—"

"Sounds complicated," Honey said.

"Not really. It's physics. Anyway, the ringers would pull the ropes, which made the headstock move, which made the bells swing and produce beautiful music. The ringers all had to be in perfect time. It was really quite a feat. And once they were going, you couldn't get away from them. They filled the air, echoing their joyous strains."

Honey looked behind her. The church steeple was almost out of sight, but even at night the white spire glowed. It shone, but it was as silent as the graveyard. Honey had never heard the bells.

"I wish they'd ring again," Honey said. "Maybe then people would want to come to our play. It would be like history in the making. What happened to them?"

Harvest let out a juicy french fry burp.

"Say excuse me, Harvest," Mary said.

Harvest giggled.

"No one really knows," Mary Moon said. "It's kind of a Sleepy Hollow mystery."

"A mystery?" Honey said. "Hum, well, I just want people to come to the play. We worked really hard, and even though I still think that I'd be a better Mary, Becky is really trying hard, and it wouldn't be right, Mom, you know if—"

"If no one came?"

"Yeah. Because of the Haunted Holiday Festival." Honey sighed. She would have to find a way. She would save Christmas!

Honey was surprised when they pulled up to the Bride of Frankenstein store. Bride of Frankenstein sold old-fashioned white wedding dresses if you asked for one, but the window display contained a black gown with gray, lacy sleeves that looked like spiderwebs. In fact, when Honey looked closer she could see that the lace had been tatted to look like spiders. She shook her head.

"What are we doing here?" Honey asked. "Who's getting married?"

"They sell more than wedding dresses," her mother said. "You can order formal clothes of all kinds here. And besides, Honey, you should know not to ask about shopping trips at Christmastime. Let me have some secrets."

Her mother split some more fries between Honey and Harvest. "I'll be right back," she said. "Don't look when you see me coming. It might ruin someone's Christmas."

As soon as the car doors were locked, Honey set her brain to figuring out exactly what gift her mother had ordered. The Moon children only got one present each on Christmas Eve. Sure, they bought each other something if they had allowance, or sometimes they made something, but from their parents, they only got one gift. Usually it was the best and most terrific gift Harry, Honey, and even Harvest, who was finally catching on to Christmas, could ever imagine. Last year, Honey got a black-and-yellow bike with a striped-bee seat. It had a horn on it that squawked loudly, and there was a custom license plate that said HONEYBEE. That was the best gift ever. So what could Mom be getting at a wedding dress shop?

Honey handed Harvest an extra-long french fry and then closed her eyes and imagined with all her imagining strength. She imagined the most beautiful dress in the world. It would be yellow but not short like little girls wore. It would be long, like a prom dress. And it wouldn't be too sparkly. And when she wore it, all her big brother's friends wouldn't think she was a snotty know-it-all. They would think she was a pretty young lady. And they would sit still and look at her when she talked, just like they did with Sarah Sinclair.

It was such a perfect Christmas present that Honey was surprised she hadn't already thought of it. She was ten years old. Of course it was time she had a formal dress of her own. She felt practically giddy at the thought.

When her mom came out of the store, Honey covered her eyes like she was supposed to. But from between her fingers she saw a flash of red fabric hanging out from the bottom of the garment bag.

Hmm. Red isn't my favorite color, but I can work with that. Honey thought. *A red formal dress is still going to be the best Christmas gift ever.*

This would be a great Christmas! In spite of the Haunted Holiday Festival.

SING-A-RING-A-LING

Miss Fortissimo was the choir teacher at Sleepy Hollow Elementary. She loved long necklaces just like she loved long notes. Today, her necklace stretched lower than her belly button. It rattled against the piano keys as she bent to play the chords that meant

STOP TALKING AND LISTEN TO YOUR TEACHER. No one ever stopped talking when they heard those notes. Ever.

She reached for the bullhorn that hung by the flag. Miss Fortissimo claimed it was a last resort, but she last-resorted three times a day. "QUIET!" she yelled through the horn. "And I mean it."

The students settled down and stopped talking.

"That's better," Miss Fortissimo said. She replaced the bullhorn on its hook. Then she leaned against the back of the piano and smiled. "We have an exciting opportunity, class. The Sleepy Hollow Elementary choir has been invited to sing at the Haunted Holiday Festival on Christmas Eve. The whole town will be there."

A couple of kiss-up girls clapped and huddled together with excited whispers. Honey rolled her eyes.

Honey gasped. "But what about the

Christmas play?" she asked. "It's on Christmas Eve too. Why would anyone want to go somewhere spooky on Christmas?"

The girls snickered and whispered louder. Jacob Norman laughed. "Because it's funner than some dumb play."

"Numbskull," Honey said. "Funner is not a word."

Miss Fortissimo glared at Honey. "That's enough, Honey Moon." Some kids chuckled like they often did when someone used Honey's full name. But she didn't care. The Christmas pageant was far more important.

"I'm talking to Mrs. Keys about canceling the play," Miss Fortissimo said. "The festival is going to be spectacular. I personally rewrote some Christmas songs to better fit with the theme." She cleared her throat and began singing while waving her hand in the air:

Silver bells, scary tales,
it's winter time in Sleepy Hollow,

Ring-a-ling, hear them scream,
soon it will be frightening . . .

Honey thought of the vampire Santa and got that fluttery feeling in her stomach again. But the feeling only made her more determined to keep the play alive. "But the Christmas program is going to be better than any haunted festival."

"What's so great about your Christmas play? Do you have scary elves? Or a vampire Santa," Jacob asked with a smirk.

"Of course not," Honey said. Sure, guys like Jacob and those silly girls would love that, but she couldn't let the Christmas play get canceled because that would mean *no* normal celebration anywhere in town, and she would be forced to sing with the school choir. And that meant she would have to attend the haunted festival. *Ugh!*

Honey peered out the window toward the town green while Miss Fortissimo sang. She had to tell them the church had something even better planned. Think fast, Honey Moon. Think fast.

"For your information, Jacob, we don't need stupid elves. We have something even better," she said. "Something splendiferous."

"Better than poisonous mistletoe?" That was Claire Sinclair, Sarah's little sister. Claire had straight, short hair that was usually hidden under a baseball cap. Today, she had on a Celtics jersey over a long-sleeved T-shirt and stylishly

25

ripped blue jeans. Claire wasn't the type to like choir, but since they wouldn't let her sign up for gym class twice a day, she'd had no choice.

That was when Isabela piped up. "I don't know, Honey. I kind of like the idea of a haunted festival. It might be fun."

Seriously? Isabela liked the idea. Honey felt like she might be teetering on being overwhelmed by everyone, but she would not be daunted. She turned her attention back to Claire.

"Mistletoe already is poisonous," Honey said, but she was losing their attention. She needed to come up with something spectacular. Something earthshaking. Something they couldn't resist. "Bells," she blurted. "We have bells. Magnificent brass bells."

Miss Fortissimo hooked her thumb in her necklace. The chain made white marks on her neck. "What are you talking about?" she asked.

Most of the class laughed. "Who cares about dumb bells?" Aiden said. Then he snorted like a pig and said, "Hey, I made a joke. Get it? Dumbbells like weightlifters . . ."

"Yes, yes, we get it." But even Miss Fortissimo couldn't contain a snicker.

Honey pointed upward as if the bell tower was right above them. "The bells in the church tower. Loud bells. Bells that rattle your bones more than any fake vampire Santa. Bells that squeeze your heart and shake your soul. Bells that are magical." She added the magical part for good measure.

21

Miss Fortissimo squinted at her. "I've lived here five years, and I've never heard bells in our town. Not those kind of bells."

"You will on Christmas Eve," Honey said. "But that's only if we have the Christmas play. Otherwise there won't be any reason to ring them."

"I saw a picture of the Liberty Bell in Washington, DC," Claire said.

"The Liberty Bell is in Philadelphia," Honey

corrected.

"But it was epic," Claire continued. "I bet a bell like that would rattle your teeth. Even with a crack in it."

"Yeah," Isabela said. "Bells might be interesting after all. I bet they'll make my dog bark like he's never barked before."

"There are twelve bells, to be precise," Honey said. "And it takes twelve people to ring them. Twelve people who have to work together in perfect harmony. It's not easy."

The murmurs were divided between excitement for the Haunted Holiday Festival and the long-silent and forgotten bells. Miss Fortissimo was not happy.

"The Haunted Holiday Festival is so boring. Same old Sleepy Hollow stuff," Honey continued. "But the ringing of the bells at Old North for the first time in years is . . . is history." Honey stood and placed her hand over her heart. "History. Like the signing of the Declaration of

Independence. Like the first astronaut to walk on the moon. Like apple pie and—"

"Baseball," said Claire.

"That's right," Honey said.

"Like ice cream," Isabela said.

That was when the class erupted with everyone talking. It sounded like a zoo had gone crazy. Miss Fortissimo snagged the bullhorn again.

"Class," she said into the horn. "Class. CLASS!"

Everyone settled. Honey had gotten so excited she had to wipe some sweat from her forehead. Maybe, just maybe she made her point. Except . . . except now she had to deliver on her promise.

Miss Fortissimo sat at the piano. "If the Christmas program gets canceled, Honey, I expect to see you at the festival. Don't forget, it'll also count as extra credit."

The day Honey needed extra credit in choir was the day she withdrew her membership from the genius club. Still, she had her way out. Unless Mrs. Keys canceled, Honey would snatch at least one holiday away from the Headless Horseman and the ghouls of Sleepy Hollow.

MUTINY

Honey hunched her shoulders and hurried past the Haunted Holiday Festival tent on her way to play practice. It was chilly, and the sky was clouding up like maybe rain was on the way.

"Hey, Honey. Whatcha doing?" Noah yelled. "You gotta come see this stuff. It's sick!"

Normally, Honey would've chatted, but she kept running. Noah was okay as far as boys went, but Honey got chills thinking about the scary stuff in that tent. Besides, after the scene she made at school, she should probably stay away from the place.

Once inside the church, she unwrapped her yellow-and-white-striped scarf and hung her coat on the pegs along the wall. Practice hadn't started yet, but everyone was getting into place. The little boy playing the cow was sitting on the steps of the stage, picking his nose and wiping boogers on the blanket in the manger. The innkeeper had his costume hiked up and was playing "hot lava" in the aisle, trying to keep his feet on the hymnals he'd scattered on the ground. Becky was painting a hay bale on the scenery wall.

Honey found her shepherd costume lying on a table with a couple of angel dresses and two leftover halos. That's when she saw the three wise men walk up to Mrs. Keys looking like they'd lost their camels.

"We're going to the Haunted Holiday Festival. That's where everyone is going," the wise men informed Mrs. Keys. They spoke in unison. *Pretty sure they rehearsed that,* Honey thought as she pulled her shepherd's costume over her blue sweater and plaid skirt.

Mrs. Keys's eyebrows lowered, making the features of her face more crowded. "But how are we going to do the play without the wise men?"

"Cancel it," Balthazar said. "Or let Scooter take a part."

"No, way!" Scooter fell back against the pew. "It's bad enough that Mom makes me come watch practice every day."

"And we want to keep the costumes until after Christmas," said Melchior. "These king costumes make great wizard outfits."

Mrs. Keys was speechless. She glanced over at Honey. Honey did her best imitation of her father's nod of encouragement.

"Everyone will be dressed up," Balthazar said, "and there'll be food trucks with burgers and fries and funnel cakes. Way better than juice and cookies."

The other kids cheered. "Funnel cakes! Hooray!"

Honey spun her shepherd's staff, wishing she could whack a wise man. Everyone couldn't quit. She didn't want to be the only one not going to the Haunted Holiday Festival.

Claire walked in. Her hair was in a short ponytail. She stood just inside the door with her hands in her pockets and cut a whistle so loud that the pipes on the organ rang. The auditorium went silent.

"Who's in charge here?" Claire asked in a voice more appropriate for coaching soccer.

Mrs. Keys's little eyes expanded. "I am, and whistling is not welcome here, young lady."

With a shrug, Claire marched down the aisle

to face Mrs. Keys. The wise men parted like they were the Red Sea. "I'm here to ring the bells," Claire said.

Honey covered her mouth. Oh no. Disaster.

"The bells?" Mrs. Keys frowned. "There are no bells in this program." She shooed the wise men away.

Becky raised her hand. "She's talking about

the church bells. You know, the ones in the steeple."

Mrs. Keys frowned even more. Honey inched forward toward Mrs. Keys. "Uh oh, I haven't exactly got permission about the bells yet. I was meaning to ask you about—"

"Honey Moon, are you trying to rewrite my script again?" Mrs. Keys asked. "One more attempt at undermining my authority and I will ban you from the performance. Or worse, I'll make you be a cow with Roger." She looked toward Roger. "Someone get that boy a tissue."

"So there aren't going to be any bells?" Claire looked at Honey. "You fibbed!"

"Honey," Becky said, "you didn't make that up, did you? What you said in school?"

"It's true. There are bells," Honey said. "I just . . . I just hadn't asked if we could ring them yet."

Claire pointed to the table full of shepherd

staffs and halos. "I don't want to be in any hokey play unless I get to do something cool like ring the bells."

Honey knew the feeling. She plucked at the ugly shepherd's robe. "What if I talked to Reverend McAdams? He might agree to let us ring the bells."

"He's on sabbatical, getting ready for the holiday season. The play will be perfect without bells," said Mrs. Keys. "And besides, only the church secretary knows where he is, and he left strict orders not to be disturbed except for an emergency."

"Look, Mrs. Keys," Honey said, "you need something to make this play more important than the festival. With all that noise outside, who is going to come in the church? We need the bells. We need to make history. Otherwise, we are wasting our time."

Mrs. Keys wasn't cooperating. Honey needed to sweeten the deal. Her eyes darted around the kids and costumes and scenery looking for a clue. Something she could bargain with. Then she saw him. Scooter. Scooter Keys doing his homework on the front row. He grimaced so hard it looked like he had just sucked ten lemons. She took a deep breath and prepared to make the ultimate sacrifice. "Here's what I'll do. In return for you letting us ring the bells, I'll help Scooter with his essay after practice."

Scooter's head popped up. "I don't need help from some fifth grader, especially a girl."

Honey sighed. He was so cute. And she was so toast.

Mrs. Keys took a deep breath and blew it out her tiny nose. "You don't even know how to find the pastor. He's at a retreat. And what if he says no?"

"I'll help Scooter anyway."

"Will not!" But Scooter's tough guy act was failing. "Mom, please. Don't make me. I can do this myself."

Mrs. Keys scratched the mole on her jaw. "It's a deal. As long as your friend here participates, bells or no bells."

Honey turned to Claire. Claire rolled her eyes. "Whatever."

And that was as close to a yes as they would get. Honey would get to hear the bells but only if she could convince Reverend McAdams, and she didn't even know where he was. But more importantly, she would have a chance at giving Sleepy Hollow a normal Christmas.

∾

After practice, Honey, Becky, Isabela, and Claire walked to Burger Heaven for milkshakes and fries.

"I can't believe you get to work with Scooter." Becky paused for another sip of her peppermint shake. "He's in eighth grade!"

"And he's good at baseball," added Claire.

Honey, Becky, and Claire often stopped at Burger Heaven before walking home after school or play practice. There was nothing like french fries after a hard day's work.

"I don't think you understand the sacrifice I'm making," said Honey. She ran her finger along the tabletop like she was doing a business presentation. "First off, Scooter is cute. True, he's a cootie-laden boy, but I know from watching everyone else in our species that I will outgrow that opinion, so looking to the future."

"You call that a sacrifice?" Becky asked.

"Awww, he's not cute," Isabela said with a slurp on her soda straw.

"I'm not finished," Honey said. "Second, as cute as he may be, he is a pain in the rear. Working with him will not be pleasant. And third, I can't rewrite the paper for him. That would be academically dishonest. Yet, I have to make it good enough that I won't be shamed if anyone hears that I'm the one who helped him."

"Blah, blah, blah," said Claire. "Get to the point." She pulled the straw from her chocolate-

banana shake and licked the ice cream off.

Honey narrowed her eyes. "Middle school boys cannot admit a girl is smarter than they are, especially one who's younger. By tutoring him, I will forever be blacklisted. He will hate my guts with all his heart."

Becky looked near tears. "I'm so sorry. I never thought of it that way. We don't have to do the bells."

"Too late," Claire exclaimed. "She promised. And now I have a plan to find this referee that you're looking for."

"Do you mean reverend?" Becky asked. "It's okay. I get confused too."

"It's my plan," said Honey. "I'm the leader here."

Claire laughed. "You're the leader? What teams are you captain of again?"

"I don't do teams," said Honey, "because I don't need a lot of people getting in my way. I can find Reverend McAdams—all by myself if I have to."

Claire flipped her ponytail over her shoulder. "Then me and Becky will just go to the Haunted Holiday Festival on Christmas Eve if that's what you want. Besides, this sounds like it's going to take a lot of sleuthing. I don't know that you have it in you. Not without our help."

Honey's fist clenched. Did anyone like Claire and her smart mouth? The way she argued and interrupted people to tell them what they were doing wrong. Sometimes being kind-hearted was more important than being a know-it-all.

"I can sleuth," Honey said. "I can sleuth with the best of them. Just call me Sherlock."

"Oh yeah? What are you getting for Christmas . . . Sherlock?"

Honey leaned over the table and crumpled a napkin in her fist. "I already know."

"What is it?"

"I'm not telling."

"You don't know," Claire said.

"Do too," said Honey.

"Then tell." Claire leaned back against the thick-cushioned booth.

"It's from Bride of Frankenstein," Honey said. "Mom told me to close my eyes when she came out of the store with it, but I peeked. It's yellow, it's satin, and I'm going to look beautiful in it, and that's all I'm saying."

"Only Scooter Keys won't speak to you anymore, so what's it matter?" Claire laughed.

"Claire," Becky said. "The bells are Honey's idea, so don't you think she should be the leader?" Becky dipped a fry in ketchup.

Claire made a loud slurping noise through her straw. Then she pinned Honey with a burning look. "We'll see how she does."

ON THE HOME FRONT

"I 'll see if he can make an appearance." Mary Moon held her cell phone between her shoulder and her ear while she bathed Harvest in the kitchen sink. "His schedule is pretty full, but he loves visiting the kids at the hospital."

Honey dropped her ratty book bag on

the table. It was a hand-me-down from Harry. Her father, John Moon, followed her inside and opened the refrigerator to grab a Boost 109 energy drink.

"I'm not going to make it 'til bedtime if I don't get some caffeine," he said.

Honey grimaced as he drank the nasty-tasting stuff. She knew because he once let her take a sip. She thought it tasted like gym socks soaked in green cough syrup.

"I wanna drink," Harvest said.

"What are you doing in the sink?" Honey asked. "Aren't you too big?"

Harvest clapped soap all over his mother.

Mary signaled in Mom sign language to keep their voices down. "Yes," she said into the phone. "He's a special boy, that's for sure." She dumped a bowl of water over Harvest's head to rinse the soap out, still clutching the phone against her ear. "I appreciate you saying that.

We are very proud of him."

Obviously, her mom was talking about Honey's big brother. Harry Moon had lived a remarkable life in his thirteen years. Magician, warrior, fighter of darkness—he was doing important stuff. She, on the other hand, was dressing like a shepherd and tutoring Scooter Keys.

"Where's Harry?" Honey mouthed.

47

Her mother ended the call with her thumb and dumped another bowl of water on Harvest. "To answer all of the questions that couldn't wait until my conversation was finished—Harvest is in the sink because he wanted to make a yogurt mishmash. He opened all the different flavors of yogurt and mixed them together . . . in my purse. It was easier to throw him in the sink and not risk dripping yogurt all over the house. It was all I could do to keep Half Moon from giving him a bath for me. That dog! As if I needed one more thing to deal with."

Honey knew her mother was frustrated, but

she couldn't help but laugh. "That would've been awesome."

Mary frowned as she pulled the plug on the sink and grabbed a towel. "Now I'm late picking Harry up from Declan's. Could this day get any crazier?"

"What's for dinner?" John Moon asked.

Mary Moon narrowed her eyes.

"I'll order pizza," he said.

She handed him the towel. "Thank you."

"And take my keys," he said. "They are yogurt free."

A quick kiss and she was gone.

John turned to Harvest, shivering in the empty sink. "C'mon, boy. Let's get you warmed up." He wrapped him in the towel and lifted him out. "Honey, grab him some clean clothes out of the laundry room, please."

Mary Moon had been putting in a lot of hours lately at her job as a nurse at Sleepy Hollow Hospital, which meant clean clothes didn't always make it to the closets and drawers. In fact, the laundry room was a good place for stashing everything. Honey had just lifted a pair of clean pajamas off the ironing board when she spotted something bright and new in the cabinet above the dryer. Something that she'd never seen before. Something in a bag. It must be a present. If she was going to be a super sleuth, she should know not just what she was getting for Christmas but what everyone in the family would get too. It'd make good practice and shut Claire up. Way to go, Sherlock.

Honey pushed her hair behind her ear and opened the door to the dryer. Then she stepped on the edge of the dryer drum and climbed on top of the machine. She paused as she heard her dad carry Harvest into the living room. She had to be very careful. Honey's knees dug into the top of the dryer as she stretched to reach the cabinet door. She opened the door and grabbed the bag. It was big. The colors were too bright for her or Harry. It must be

49

something for Harvest. The bag crinkled, and Honey froze. John Moon sang in the living room, and Harvest giggled. Quickly, she pushed the bag aside . . . and came face-to-face with a gross monster.

Big googly eyes rolled. A sharp snout pointed at her beneath a bald green head. It was like a nightmare toy for babies. She couldn't drop it fast enough.

"Honey, did you forget?" her dad called.

She hopped off the dryer. The thing was supposed to be a turtle. She could see it now that she was away from it. But it was deflated. Empty. Probably from one of those stores that helped you stuff it full of fluff. She grabbed the deflated thing and shoved it in the bag and then climbed back up the dryer again. It was ugly, but with the bright colors and goofy eyes, Harvest would love it. She put the bag back in the cabinet, closed the door, and hurried into the living room with the polka dot pj's.

Honey tossed her father the pajamas. "Here

you go."

He caught them just before they flew over his head. "Thanks."

"Dad, where is Reverend McAdams this week? I need to talk to him."

"Really? What is it, Honey? Maybe I can answer your questions."

Honey flopped onto the couch and hugged a pillow. "I'm wondering about the bells. At Old North. Mom said they used to ring."

51

John pulled up the zipper on Harvest's pj's. "That's right, they did, didn't they? I'd forgotten."

"Well, I need to talk to Reverend McAdams. Mrs. Keys said we could ring the bells at the Christmas play, but I have to get his permission."

"Reverend McAdams is taking a break. That means he can't be bothered." He blew a raspberry into Harvest's neck. "Except for an emergency."

"I don't want to bother him. He just needs to say yes or no. Yes, really, and then I won't have to bother him for as long. Isn't that what he's supposed to do? Answer questions and help people? Can't be a reverend if you don't want people bothering you . . ."

Her father had stopped wrestling with Harvest and gave Honey a look that spoke volumes. She had crossed the line.

"Fine," she said. She buried her face into the pillow, which oddly enough smelled like root beer. Once Honey settled on a goal, there wasn't much else she could think about until she'd accomplished it. And the best way to make progress on a goal was to set a deadline. That's what her life coach told her. Well, she didn't have a life coach, but as soon as she could afford it, she'd hire one. Or be one. But a time limit was set. December 24. Ringing bells on December 26 wouldn't be the same. She needed to find the reverend. Now.

"Stop your grumbling," her dad said. "Yep, I hear you grumbling even if you didn't say anything. Go clean all that yogurt out of your mom's purse. She's been working hard and could use the break."

Honey tossed the pillow on the couch and dragged herself to the kitchen. She plugged the empty sink and then took her mom's purse and turned it upside down. The tissue, gum, and receipts clumped together. Even the loose change went *splat* instead of *clink*. Honey had to shake the purse hard to get everything to fall out of it—including her mother's wallet. She grabbed a paper towel and picked up the keys to clean them. Her mom's ID from the hospital was next. And the gum . . . well, it tasted pretty good with a coating of yogurt mishmash.

Her dad was on the phone ordering pizza when her mom and Harry walked in. Her big brother came to stand by her and looked into the sink.

"Get out of my air," she said. He hadn't done anything to her, but if she didn't bicker, he'd think something was wrong.

"Not now, Honey," he said.

53

Mary Moon stood in the doorway, waiting for John Moon to get off the phone. Her eyes were blotchy. Her nose red. Something was wrong. Harry only shrugged.

John Moon finished his call. "What happened to you?"

"I was late picking Harry up, so I had to hurry. And then . . ."

Harvest walked into the room holding his dad's Boost 109.

"You let him drink your energy drink? Are you crazy? Do you know what that'll do? Now we'll be up all night. I've been working day and night—"

"Calm down, Mary," John Moon said.

But saying calm down to Honey's mom was like throwing gas on a flame.

"Calm down? Why? Because there's no reason for me to be upset? I shouldn't mind that my two-year-old will be up all night and I'll barely get any sleep before working another shift? I should be happy that I got pulled over for speeding in a school zone . . . after hours . . . and that I didn't have my license, because I didn't have my wallet because my purse is ruined? I should be thrilled!"

Honey stepped closer to Harry. She leaned until her shoulder bumped against him. Her mom didn't do so well when she was sleepy. A

55

quick nap and she'd be a new person, but the whole family knew to stay out of her way until then.

"Go take a break," John said. "You're tired. I'll feed the kids."

She nodded and stumbled off. John took the drink from Harvest and ruffled his hair. "I'm the one who needs energy, not you." Harvest grinned, unaware of the trouble he'd caused.

"What did the police say?" Honey asked Harry.

"It happened before she got to me." He looked at the yogurt-coated coins, receipts, and keys in the sink. "Wow. Harvest did that?" He elbowed her. "I guess having *three* perfect children was too much to ask."

Honey felt warm all over. Her big brother had called her perfect. As much as she pestered Harry, she liked it when he said nice things to her.

Jail House Rock

"**A**re we going to the court house now?" Honey tossed her stained backpack behind the console of the minivan next to Harvest's car seat. "I'll see criminals, won't I? I can ask them what they're in for. I bet they're all guilty . . ."

"Stop, Honey Moon." Her mother did not

look excited. "Your job is to keep a hold of Harvest while I pay my ticket. Do not talk to anyone in there. Do you understand? The people there have broken the law."

"Like you?" Honey asked.

Her mother kept her eyes straight ahead, reached over, and cranked up the radio.

58

No one could communicate while Harvest's nursery rhyme CD blared over the speakers. Harvest rocked his car seat while mumbling along. Honey didn't want to talk anyway. She had less than twenty-four hours before the next play practice, and she had to muster all her sleuthing skills. She had to find Reverend McAdams and get permission to ring the bells. She wanted happy Christmas carols, not dungeon sounds.

They pulled into a parking lot with a bunch of police cruisers and looked for an empty spot. Mary Moon got the last open space. She unbuckled Harvest, gathered her purse, and took a deep breath like she was about to dive off the high-dive.

"Let's go," she said.

They made it inside the courthouse, past the metal detector and the guards, before Harvest got fidgety and tried to run away. Honey saw that he had his sights on a large potted plant. The last thing her mom needed was for Harvest to dig in the dirt. Honey took his hand. "Come on, Harvest. Let's sit on the bench. Your mama is doing her best to stay out of jail. She doesn't need you destroying county property."

There was a line of people standing in front of a window with bars. Behind the window, Honey got a glimpse of a woman who looked way too old to be chasing bad guys. A sand-colored bench stretched almost the length of the wall, only leaving room for a square end table full of pamphlets and a dish of butterscotch candy.

Honey lifted Harvest to the bench and got him a piece of candy to pass the time while her mom waited in line. A big teenager came to the back of the line with his dad and stood in front of her. The back of his dad's jacket read Hugo's Repair. He never lifted his eyes from his smart phone even though his dad was talking to him.

"You're lucky it wasn't worse," the dad whispered. "You could've killed someone, driving like that."

Honey scooted Harvest closer against her. A real live criminal, well sort of criminal, was standing in front of her, although he didn't look so dangerous while texting and getting lectured by his dad.

"How would you live with yourself if that had happened?" the dad asked. "Ever think of that?"

"Relax, Dad. Chill," the boy said. His thumbs never stopped tapping on his phone. "Nothing happened. Just a little ticket and some body work. Nothing your boys at the garage can't handle."

His dad's skin turned red above the collar of his green jacket. He muttered under his breath. "There's no such thing as a little ticket. You don't appreciate how hard I work for this money, and don't get me started on the repairs."

But the boy didn't seem to be impressed. Honey's jaw clenched. How could a boy . . . maybe as much as ten years older than she . . . not take responsibility for his actions? She wanted to grab his phone and stomp on it, but there was a police officer sitting nearby. Stomping phones was probably illegal.

The officer saw her looking at him. He creaked as he left his chair and sat next to her on the bench. All the hardware on his belt jangled against the wooden bench and kept him leaning forward. Was she in trouble?

"May I help you, young lady?"

Harvest stared up at him with golf-ball-sized eyes. Honey patted his leg and left her hand there for comfort—hers and his.

"No. I don't need anything," Honey nearly whispered. "Just waiting on my mom." Then gathering her courage she asked, "On second thought, I'm wondering how this money thing works. When people break the law, they have to pay a fine. Is that right?"

The police officer nodded. "Yes, ma'am. Most tickets don't require jail time, just money. Otherwise they wouldn't take the offense seriously."

As this boy wasn't. He was too busy on his phone to notice that his dad had slipped away, leaving him standing in line alone.

Harvest smacked a sticky hand on Honey's knee, but at least he hadn't got her wool skirt or knee socks dirty. She grabbed another butterscotch for him and unwrapped the golden wrapper.

"I have another question," she said. "What if you were trying to find someone who was hiding out for a little while? What would be the best way to see where they went?"

"First thing we do is run their credit cards and look for their phone signal."

"How do I do that?" she asked.

"You can't. That's police work."

Honey rubbed her chin. Seeing how she probably couldn't get the police to track down the reverend when he hadn't broken any laws, she'd have to try another way.

"But what if it was a friend?"

"Why wouldn't your friend tell you where she was going?" the officer asked.

"You have no imagination," Honey said.

The officer laughed. "Alright, missy. Let's say your friend left town without telling you. Assuming she's old enough to travel alone, I'd recommend that you get on her computer and see what she's been looking at online. Airlines? Passport information? Hotels?"

Honey frowned. Computer? How on earth could she get to Reverend McAdams's computer?

"If you don't have access to her computer, then look for a paper trail. Has she got fliers for resorts? Bills from travel agents? Bids on airfares? Rarely does someone pack up and leave without doing some preparation, and most of the time they leave behind evidence."

"Yes," Honey said. "Evidence." Just what Sherlock always looked for.

The officer smiled.

Reverend McAdams's office held the key. Without the reverend, there'd be no bells. And without the bells, no one would want to come to the Christmas play. And without the Christmas play, Honey would have to go to the Haunted Holiday Festival. If she could just get in the reverend's office . . .

The line moved forward again, but new people continued to file in at the back. The boy was nearly to the front of the line when her mother came toward her, putting her wallet in her purse. Her eyebrows rose at seeing Honey's companion.

"I'm sorry, Officer Taft. Has she been a problem?" she asked.

The police officer stood. "Not at all. I enjoy helping a fellow detective."

Her mother shot her a questioning look. Honey shrugged as the line of offenders moved forward and the woman behind the glass yelled at the teenager.

65

"Put that phone away and answer me. What are you here for?"

The young man startled. "I'm Hugo Gillis, Junior. I'm here to pay a ticket."

With a few taps of her keyboard, her eyes narrowed. "What a nice contribution to the county's finances. You're very generous. Pay up."

The boy turned from left to right. Then he spun a complete circle. "Dad? Dad? Where are you?"

"C'mon on, boy. I don't have all day," she said. "Get your wallet out and pay."

"You gotta be kidding me!" he nearly yelled. "I don't have that kind of money. Where's my dad?"

"Your dad's name isn't on this citation. He wasn't the one who broke the law. You are. You don't pay then you're a wanted man. Might as well turn yourself in now and save us the trouble of hunting you down. Sergeant, could you help over here with this young man?" The woman looked at the officer who had been talking to Honey.

"Let's go, kid." The officer took his arm.

Honey's mother bumped her with her knee. "Do you know anything about this?"

Honey could only watch with her mouth hanging open. That phone had been the most important thing in the boy's life a minute ago. Now he would've gladly passed it over to the clerk if he could only see his father again.

"Wait." The clerk's fingers flew over her keyboard. "There's been a mistake. It seems that his fine has already been paid." She looked up in amazement. "Today's your lucky day."

"Are you sure?" the officer said.

"Paid in full. His debt is forgiven." And the clerk didn't look like she believed it.

The officer released his arm. "Wow, kid. I don't know who loved you enough to do that, but you're free. Merry Christmas."

Honey turned to see the boy's father waiting by the door. He hadn't left him after all.

"There's more Christmas here than in the entire Haunted Holiday Festival," Honey said.

Her mother picked up Harvest. "Sometimes, child, you say the most unusual things. Now, let's go home."

HOME RUN

"What are you doing at Claire's house?" Honey dropped her book bag on her bed without lowering her phone and kicked off her shoes. This was the only day of the week they didn't have play practice, and she'd thought Becky would come to her house. It was still early. Just about three o'clock.

"Hanging out. You can come too."

Honey flopped on her bed. She didn't want to go to Claire's house. She wanted Becky to go with her so they could snoop in Reverend McAdams's office. Mrs. Clementine, his secretary, would let Becky in. Everyone trusted Becky. Honey, not so much.

"We've got work to do. Tell Claire you have to go."

"That's not nice. Besides, her big sister Sarah is going to do my makeup. I can't wait. Mom said I could even try a little mascara."

Honey rolled her eyes. Claire didn't give a flea's life savings for looking pretty, but Becky would love it.

"Listen, Becky. Sarah can do that later. I need your help. We have to find Reverend McAdams."

There was a long pause until Becky finally said, "Ummm, Honey. I don't know if I'm going to be in the play. Miss Fortissimo offered me a solo in the choir's Haunted Holiday performance. I'm going to sing "Have Yourself a Scary Little Christmas." It's going to be great."

Honey flopped onto her stomach and held herself up by her elbows. "You're going to the Haunted Holiday Festival? For real? Doesn't the word friendship mean anything to you? Doesn't the word commitment mean anything? How could you do this?" She felt nearly sick to her stomach. Becky knew how important the Christmas pageant was to her. Was this what betrayal felt like?

"Let me ask Claire," Becky said and then the phone went dead. Honey glanced at the screen. Less than a two-minute call and she'd lost her temper with her best friend. Or was Becky her best friend anymore? Seemed like all she wanted to do was hang out with Claire.

Her phone buzzed. A text from Becky.

N. Church 5 min omw

Honey hopped off the bed, grabbed her

shoes, and ran into the living room. "I'm going to pageant practice with Becky," she said.

Her mother looked up for the stack of Christmas cards she was signing. "There's no practice this afternoon."

"We're going to work on something for the play by ourselves," Honey said. Which was true, in a way.

"Do you want me to drive you?"

"No, thanks." Honey grabbed her coat and hurried out the door. She was on the church grounds before she slowed down. Claire and Becky were waiting for her.

"You're late," Claire said. She tossed a dirty snowball from hand to hand.

Honey was out of breath. "I got here as quick as I could."

"You'd never make it in baseball," Claire said. "Tagged out on first base every time."

Honey glared. "There are more important things than baseball."

"There are more important things than hearing bells ring," Claire said.

Becky stepped between them. "What do you need us to do, Honey?"

"I thought you wanted to sing at the festival." Honey was trying hard not to sound upset. Especially in front of Claire.

"I do," Becky said. "But I don't want the play to be canceled, either."

"Well, we need to get into Reverend McAdams's office to investigate. Then once we figure out where he is, we need to call him about the bells."

"Why don't you just ask where he is?" Claire said.

"Because they won't tell me. And if I ask to go in his office, then they'll know I'm up to something. That's why I need Becky. No one will suspect her."

"Am I going to get in trouble?" Becky chewed on a long brown curl.

Honey shook her head. "You just get us in his office. We aren't going to hurt anything."

Becky tapped her finger on her chin. "I did draw a pretty picture of North Church. Well, I copied it from a picture." She dug through her backpack and pulled out a folded piece of card stock. As promised, there was a beautiful picture of the steeple at night surrounded by the Sleepy Hollow town.

"I'll tell Mrs. Clementine I want to hang it in his office to surprise him when he gets back."

"And what am I supposed to do?" Claire asked.

"We don't need you," Honey said. "No one invited you, anyway."

"But she promised to be in the play." Becky smoothed out the picture. "She's part of the team."

How long before they could make teams again? When was the next election because Honey didn't remember casting a vote?

"Well, I'm the captain," Honey said. "We'll be back." And she and Becky darted into the side entrance that led to the offices.

"Hello, girls." The secretary, a tall woman with red hair, put her weight into a giant paper cutter. The handle sliced through the stack of red paper with a bone-chilling whisk. "How can I help you?"

Becky held up her picture. "I made this for Reverend McAdams, and I want to hang it in his office. When he gets back, he'll be so surprised! He loves my drawings."

The secretary moved the paper around for the next cut. "Just leave it on my desk, and I'll put it in there."

Becky blinked her big brown eyes. Honey was impressed. She could never fake that level of hurt and innocence. "But I want it to be special. I want to hang it right behind his computer."

"And that's where I'll put it. He'll see it first thing. Goodbye, girls."

She left no room for arguing. Becky dragged her feet to the door. The secretary paused, looking straight at Honey through her glasses, which had slipped down her pointy nose. She didn't even blink until Honey had reached the door.

Fail. Big fat fail.

"Whaddya find out?" Claire tossed the snowball up and caught it with her bare hand.

"Nothing," Honey said. "She didn't let us in."

"What kind of church is this?" Claire asked.

"One that doesn't give children unlimited

access to the pastor's study," Honey said.

"Now that you mention it," Becky replied, "I guess I can't blame her. It is the reverend's private office."

"You know, this snowball is more ice than snow." Claire squeezed it hard. "It'd raise a welt if I threw it at you."

"Then let's not do that." On the best of days, Honey wasn't the most patient person. Today, of all days, she shouldn't have to deal with Claire.

"That window there." Claire pointed. "Is that the pastor's office?"

"What of it?" Honey asked. "I'm sure it's locked too."

"Be right back." Claire dashed off to the garden shed in the corner of the courtyard and returned with a snow shovel. "You want in that office?"

Honey's pulse picked up. She looked at the shovel, then at the girl with the baseball cap. There were times you knew you were making a deal with the devil, but in this case, she was making a deal to save Christmas, which wasn't the same thing.

"What are you going to . . ."

Claire tossed the snowball straight up in the cold air, swung the shovel like a baseball bat, and *bam!* hit it with the shovel like she was an all-star slugger. The ball of ice flew like a comet directly toward the church office. Straight as an arrow to the window.

"Noooo!" hollered Honey. But it was too late. It hit with a smack. Glass shattered. Shards mixed with the dirty snow melting on the ground beneath.

Claire tapped the shovel against the sole of her tennis shoe. "You can thank me later."

ON A MISSION

The damage was done. No use crying over spilt milk or, in this case, broken glass. Plans formed and re-formed as Honey tried to figure out how to best use this to their advantage. But she had to think fast. It wouldn't be long before Mrs. Clementine came outside to look for the culprit.

The door flew open. "What just happened?" The secretary stepped outside holding her sweater tightly around her shoulders. She turned to look at the church. Her mouth dropped open. "Did you do this?"

Claire removed her cap. "It's my fault. I'm sorry. Let me help you clean it up."

Becky knelt in the snow and gingerly picked up a piece of glass. "Do you have a trash bin out here?"

Honey raced to the door. "I'll clean the office."

Not waiting for the secretary to stop her, she ran into the building, darted past the secretary's desk, and ran down the short hall to the reverend's office. Once there, she had a moment of misgiving. The only time she'd even been in Reverend McAdams's office was with her parents. They'd visited a lot when all that strange stuff started happening to Harry. I mean, what would you do if your son suddenly could do magic . . . real magic? Wouldn't you want to talk to someone that was in good with God? And every time they visited, it was a serious occasion—be on your best behavior, no gum, sit up straight in the chair, and all that good stuff.

What would her parents think of her going inside without Reverend McAdams's permission? If that were a test question, Honey knew the answer, but sacrifices had to be made.

"Sorry, Rev," she whispered as she eased the door open. Besides the light from the recently opened window, it was dark. Heavy shadows stretched from a hall tree across the bookcases. No light came from the computer screen. Not eerie, really. More weighty. Like the room was watching her but only for her own good.

81

Honey walked behind the desk. She'd never been on this side of it before. She looked at the two chairs where her family had sat to talk about Harry. They'd pulled up the chair from the corner, and she'd stood behind her dad. From the pastor's view, the room didn't look nearly as intimidating. The clock was cleverly placed on the opposite wall so he could keep on schedule without them knowing he was checking the time. Smart man. And she had to find him.

The desk was clean, marred only by a block of sticky notes and an old-fashioned phone with a lot of buttons and a cord. Behind the desk, against the wall, sat the computer and her best chance at finding the reverend. Fliers, mail, jotted notes, and even a row of Hot Wheels cars littered this area. That made her pause. The learned reverend collected toy cars? Hmmm. Forcing herself to forget the distractions, she got back to business and flipped through the paper. Pages of notes scribbled on legal pads, lists of people and hospital names, a thank-you card from a church member—lots of correspondence but nothing about a vacation.

Honey couldn't help but feel guilty, but she kept telling herself she was doing good. To turn people away from the festival and toward a normal Christmas celebration would be a good thing.

Footsteps sounded in the hall. Honey spun

in the spinning chair and grabbed the trashcan out from beneath the desk. Holding it in one hand, she threw herself on the floor and managed to get a few pieces of glass in the trashcan before Mrs. Clementine came to the door.

"Just get the big pieces," she said. "I'll vacuum up the rest."

"Are you going to call him?" Honey asked. "Doesn't he need to know about his office window being broken?"

"We're not to interrupt him unless it's an emergency," she said. "Do you think a broken window is an emergency? After the potluck salmonella poisoning, I can assure you this is not an emergency."

Honey picked up the melting snowball and tossed it out the window.

"Hey," Claire yelled from outside. "Be careful. You might hit something."

Now she was worried?

The secretary inspected the window frame. Shards of glass hung in the frame like jagged shark teeth. "I'll get the maintenance man to fix it. He'll patch it up until we can get the glass company out." She turned to Honey. "And I'm afraid I will have to call your parents. It might be an accident, but word will get out. Better for them to have heard it from me."

That was debatable, but Honey wouldn't argue. She reached over the trashcan to drop more glass in when a picture caught her eye. There among the Tootsie Roll wrappers was a brochure featuring a couple on a porch overlooking the ocean.

Cape Sanctuary Bed & Breakfast—Because Life was Meant to be Appreciated

Honey grabbed the corner of the brochure and shook off the glass. She flipped it over to the back. The phone number was circled.

BINGO!

Thank you, Officer Taft.

Mrs. Clementine was saying something about her cutting herself and getting an infection, but Honey didn't care. She'd found what she was looking for. It was time to go. She nodded and slipped the card beneath the trashcan. Then, using the trashcan to shield her treasure, she carried the can back to its place under the desk. By the time she stood up again, the travel brochure was safely in her pocket.

"Sorry again about the window," Honey said on her way outside as she rushed to huddle with the girls.

They ran a safe distance from the church into the town green past the tent. Becky dusted the snow off a bench, and they sat together.

"Mission accomplished," Honey said. "I found him." She produced the brochure and pointed to the number. "All we got to do is call him. He'll say we can ring the bells, and then they'll have to keep the Christmas play going."

"Do you think the bells will make that much of a difference?" Becky tucked her hands inside her pockets and shivered.

Somehow this was already about more than hearing some bells. It was about the way Miss Fortissimo had so easily dismissed their Christmas play. Oh, you have a play? That's too bad because the Haunted Holiday Festival is going to be even better. It was about the way that all the shiny, golden warmth of Christmas had turned into cold, dull metal in Sleepy Hollow. Instead of a Christmas tree on the town square, there was a Headless Horseman covered in orange lights. Instead of cheerful yard decorations, there were scary angels and creepy snowmen. Blood-thirsty, dark songs took the place of peace on Earth, goodwill to men. Not that the scary wasn't funny sometimes, but she couldn't find the true Christmas love in Sleepy Hollow anywhere.

Honey shrugged. "We won't know until we try." She took out her phone and punched the numbers.

"Hello, this is Honey Moon. I'm looking for Reverend— No, I don't need to book my honeymoon. I'm only ten. My name is Honey. Honey Moon. Is the Reverend— Yes, my parents are so clever. Have you thought about what I live with?" At least she didn't have to tell them that her brothers were named Harry and Harvest. "What I need is to talk to Reverend McAdams. Is he available?"

What followed was some hemming and hawing as the woman explained that she wasn't supposed to disturb Mr. McAdams, but soon a very familiar voice came over the line. Honey could hardly believe it. Butterflies congregated in her stomach.

"Honey Moon, how did you get my number?"

"Hello, Reverend. I have an important question about the Christmas Eve service." She pulled herself up to her full height. "You see, I'm helping Mrs. Keys work out the details for the Christmas Eve play, and we were wondering—"

"I'm on a sabbatical to prepare for the

new year. Mrs. Clementine was not to give this number to anyone."

"And I won't give it to anyone, either. Well, no one besides Becky and Claire. You don't know Claire. She doesn't go to church, and she spits like a boy and loves baseball more than anything. And, boy, can she hit. But what we were wondering was if we could ring the bells for the Christmas Eve play. You know, how they used to?" Honey tapped the phone onto speaker so Becky and Claire could hear.

There was a long pause. Finally he spoke again. "Of course you can ring bells, shake tambourines, toot a flute. Whatever Mrs. Keys decides."

"No, I mean the big bells in the steeple. Those are the bells we want to ring."

He took a deep breath. "I see. While I appreciate your enthusiasm, as well as your ingenuity in finding my phone number, ringing those bells is impossible. That belfry is over four hundred years old. The boards are rotten. The stairs are rickety. It's not safe to go up there. We can't be responsible for what happens. Get some jingle bells if you'd like, but the church bells have to stay silent. They're just not safe."

To Tutor Scooter

Honey clicked off her phone and stared at the blank screen. "I can't believe it. How can he say no? How can he want them to stay quiet?"

Becky craned her head back and followed the lines of the steeple up. "I'm glad we called him. We could get hurt going up there. Can you imagine if those bells crashed to the ground? That would be a total disaster."

"I'm not afraid," Claire said. "I'd still do it."

Honey studied the tall structure. She was afraid. She couldn't even pretend that she wasn't, but she'd go anyway. She'd go because she was afraid, but she was more afraid of having the Haunted Holiday Festival be the only Christmas celebration in Sleepy Hollow.

"I've got a plan," she said. She dropped her phone into her book bag and studied the steeple. The glass windows reflected the late afternoon light back at her. It was impossible to see inside them. Were they painted or boarded up? It didn't matter. She'd know soon enough.

"We have practice tomorrow night," Honey said. "That's when we're going into the belfry."

"Awesome!" said Claire.

"We can't," said Becky. "Mrs. Keys will never

let us."

"We aren't going to ask," said Honey. The final details were falling into place even as she spoke. "After practice, we sneak away from everyone else, and we hide. We wait until Mrs. Keys leaves and then we climb up into the belfry. If we each bring a flashlight . . ."

"Wait," said Claire. "Won't our mothers be waiting on us after practice? They'll come looking for us."

"Let's use your sister," Honey said. Claire's big sister Sarah used to babysit Harry. Now, with Harry being thirteen, they were allowed to be home by themselves for short periods of time unless their mother was working all day, and then, Harvest's nanny stayed. "Let's have Sarah pick us up. We'll tell her that we're staying afterwards to practice something. She won't come until later, and we'll have time to check it out."

Becky chewed on an already nubby fingernail. Claire swung one arm around as if practicing for fast-pitch softball. She pretend lobbed a ball directly at one of the port-a-potties that had been set up along the street for the big event. The girls also saw generators and picnic tables being set up along with vendor booths and craft displays. It looked like fun if it weren't for the terrifying decorations.

"I'll ask her," Claire said. "I'll tell her to pick us up thirty minutes after practice. That should give us time."

"But what are we hoping to find?" Becky asked. "If it's too dangerous . . ."

"What if it's not as dangerous as he thinks?" asked Honey. "Or what if it's easy to fix? Why couldn't the church get a carpenter to fix the stairs? But we need to know first. Then we can ask for help."

"In the meantime," said Claire, "I'm working on my Haunted Holiday costume. I'm going to be a melting Frosty the Snowman. Becky's mom is making me a skinny snowman suit with bones sticking out, and it'll leak water everywhere as I go. I'm going to cry, 'I'm melting, I'm melting,' just like the witch in *The Wizard of Oz*."

Honey tucked her escaping shirttails into her pleated skirt. And she'd thought the shepherd costume was bad.

"As long as you both think it's safe . . ." Becky said. "I think Mom will let Sarah bring me home. She likes your sister."

Everyone liked Sarah. Especially Harry. He was in love with her. But he was thirteen, and Sarah was sixteen. Three years was way too big of a difference. Honey frowned. Then again, Scooter was thirteen, and she was ten. Somehow that didn't seem as bad.

Scooter!

"I'm supposed to be at Mrs. Keys's tonight!" Honey jumped from the bench. "I forgot I have to help Scooter."

95

Honey ran all the way to Mrs. Keys's house. By the time she arrived, her sock had bunched up inside her sneaker, and she was sweaty beneath her coat. After ringing the doorbell, she bent to tug on her sock, but the wrinkle wouldn't leave. Mrs. Keys answered the door.

Honey could not contain her enthusiasm. "I spoke to Reverend McAdams."

"You did?" Mrs. Keys said. "But how—"

"Don't worry about it," Honey said. "The important thing is that we're working on the bells."

"Honey Moon," Mrs. Keys said, "you are a caution."

Honey smiled, mostly on the inside. "Oh, let's just say I'm good at writing essays *and* at sleuthing."

Mrs. Keys led Honey to a dining room table covered in costumes. She lifted a quilted sewing box off and pushed the costumes to the side. "Scooter, Honey is here. Bring your essay."

Honey took a seat in the fancy high-backed chair. Would he really hate her forever? She thought of his mean comments during practice and braced for the worst.

Scooter strutted down the stairs and into the dining room. His athletic pants swished with each step. His dark hair dripped, and he smelled good. He must have just got out of the shower after basketball practice.

Harry had such cool friends.

"Here's my paper." He shoved three crumpled pages toward her and moved the next chair as far away as he could. "I didn't have much time to work on it. I'm going to do it better before I turn it in and all, but I've been busy lifting weights and shooting baskets." His eyes never left the table.

Honey picked up the paper. When Scooter was at her house hanging out with Harry, he always ignored her. Now he had to pay attention, but she hadn't thought about exactly what she was going to say to him. What if his

paper was awful? She didn't want to make him feel stupid.

She scanned over it. Couldn't concentrate. Tried again. What was it even about?

"Tell me when you're done," he said. And he got up and went into the kitchen.

Honey gripped the paper. From the kitchen she recognized the familiar voice of his mother arguing with her son.

Scooter said, "She's grading it now. She's not thirsty. She just got here."

Honey licked her lips. Actually she was thirsty, but that would have to wait. The paper was a compare and contrast. That was easy enough. And his topic was ninjas versus gladiators. Honey settled in as she read. Besides covering a boring topic, it wasn't that bad. It just needed some work on the structure. Scooter stepped into the room with a sneer on his face and two Cokes in hand.

99

"Here. Mom said you are thirsty."

Honey didn't even touch the can. Instead, she held out the paper. "This is good," she said. "You did a good job in the introduction telling why ninjas and gladiators were both epic warriors."

"I did?" He sat. "Well, it is important. Gotta give respect where it's due."

"And you give a lot of descriptions about what makes their different fighting styles unique, but what would make the paper move from a C to an A would be the structure of the paper."

Scooter grabbed a pen and a blank piece of paper from his folder. "What do you mean?"

He was listening to her. Scooter Keys was treating her like she was thirteen. Or at least twelve.

"In the paragraphs following the intro, describe how ninjas and gladiators are alike— training, fighting with swords, taking on more than one enemy at a time. Don't talk about any differences yet. Then, once you've written about everything you can think of, start over with ways they are different."

He took the paper. "I thought I did both in here, already."

"But keep them separate," she said. "Compare first, how they are the same, and once you've done that, then contrast. You have that in here, but it's mashed together like yogurt."

"What?" Scooter said.

"Never mind," Honey said.

Scooter's pen moved on the blank page. "That should be easy enough," he said. "I can cut and paste this, then read through . . ."

From the other room they could hear the front door opening. Scooter ticked off sentences from his first draft. "Thanks, Honey. I didn't know what to expect."

"Scooter? What's going on here? What are you doing?"

Honey looked up. It was her brother Harry. He made a face like he'd just caught a whiff of Harvest's dirty diaper.

Scooter grabbed his papers and shoved them into his book bag. "Finally! I'm tired of babysitting your bratty sister. Take her home."

Honey couldn't stop blinking. Harry couldn't stop laughing.

"Mom told me she was here working on homework with you, but I didn't believe her. The day Honey needs help from you on homework —well, I know she's faking it. She probably asked for help just because she thinks you're C-U-T-E."

Honey jumped to her feet. "Shut up, Harry! I did not ask for help. I . . . I . . ." There was Scooter looking like he'd just swallowed a worm and it was crawling back up his throat. She couldn't tell Harry that Scooter needed her help. He'd bug Scooter about it forever. She crossed her arms and stomped her foot. "I'm going home. And if you tell anyone, I'll make sure everyone knows you sleep with that stuffed rabbit."

She grabbed her coat and book bag and stomped out of the house. She would never speak to Harry again. Harry would get the silent treatment for the rest of the week.

Harry ran down the street after her. "Leave my friends alone," he said. "It's creepy for you to go to their house. He won't hang out with me anymore if you keep this up."

"Shut up," she said. "You don't know anything."

"I know when my little sister is stepping on my turf. What would you say if you went to Becky's and found Harvest there playing blocks with her? Wouldn't you be mad?"

Harvest would be better than Claire. Honey already felt like she was losing her friend.

103

"You're so busy with all your magic shows and appearances you don't have time for your friends anyway."

"That's not true. Scooter, Bailey, Declan, and Hao all hang out with me. I include them."

But he didn't include her. And sometimes it hurt.

104

A Most Dangerous Quest

"Are they gone yet?" Becky's muffled voice sounded from beneath a table while Claire lay on her side, her knees pulled in like she was a pill bug. Play practice had just ended, and the girls were waiting for everyone to leave.

Honey peeked out the window. "Mrs. Keys

is still in the parking lot. Don't turn on any flashlights yet." Her heart raced a little because she was thinking that maybe, just maybe, she should be worried about the bells. What if Reverend McAdams had all the right info? She looked back at her friends, and yes, she mostly considered Claire to be her friend. She just wasn't sure she was ready to share Becky with her. But there they all were, planning together to ring the bells. Now that's something only true friends plan to do together. Claire was going to wear a melty Frosty the Snowman costume for the Haunted Holiday Festival, but maybe it was really Honey who was doing some melting. Her heart, anyway. She heard a car door slam and lifted her nose above the window sill. The lot was empty.

"Everyone is gone," Honey called. "Let's go."

Switching their flashlights on, the girls crawled out of hiding and hurried to the big arch at the front of North Church. Several white paneled doors lined the room. One went to the basement and one to the coat closet, but there was one that they had never seen opened. There was a sign on it that read NOT AN EXIT.

Honey twisted the brass door knob. It clattered as it rotated round and round uselessly. "It's broken."

Claire traced the door with her beam of light. "Up there. Those nails are bent to hold the door closed."

"I know what to get." Becky dashed off, her flashlight beam bouncing.

107

Maybe having Claire around wasn't so bad. Honey wouldn't have wanted to wait by herself. She hated being alone, especially with the wicked statues visible from the Haunted Holiday in the next lot.

"This is a blast," Claire said. "I've never broke into a building before."

Were they criminals? Was Honey the ringleader?"

"We have to try and save the season," she

explained, making the excuse to herself as much as to Claire. "It's a good cause."

In a few minutes, Becky returned with a butter knife from the kitchen. Becky tried to reach the nails, but even standing on her tiptoes, she couldn't reach.

"No problem," Honey said looking at Claire. "You can get on your hands and knees and be like a step stool."

"Me? Why not you?"

"'Cause I'm the leader."

"Ugh." But Claire bent down and let Becky stand on her back anyway. "Hurry," Claire said. "You're heavy."

Becky used the knife to pry a nail and slowly straighten it. Another nail. And another nail and . . ."

"Finish!" cried Claire. "I'm going to fall!"

Becky pried the last nail and jumped from

Claire's back just in time because Claire went *splat* on the floor like a belly flopper.

"Sorry," Becky said.

But Honey was already pulling the door open. Cobwebs covered the opening. A few bulletins littered the floor, the top one from a 1994 service. Becky took the knife, punctured the web, and dragged it down.

"Ewww," Honey said.

109

"They're just spiders." Becky swung the knife around, but the sticky web wouldn't fall.

Claire shined the light on the ancient stairs disappearing up into the dark, narrow opening. "Let's do this."

"Ready?" Honey asked.

"Ready," Claire and Becky replied.

Honey stepped on the first step. It felt only a little rickety under her foot. "I think we should go one at a time," she said. "The steps might not hold all of us at the same time."

"Good thinking," Becky said.

Honey climbed the stairs like she was walking over glass, trying to stay on her toes. She shined the light up and was finally able to see the bell-ringing room. The old, dusty smell made her nose itch. She coughed and sneezed once so loudly all three girls held their breath in case of an avalanche.

Honey reached the top and stumbled once as her toe got caught in a knothole. "It's okay," she called. "I'm safe. Come on up."

Becky and Claire followed and soon they were all standing in the belfry. They shined their lights around at the long, thick, and heavy ropes used to pull the bells.

"Wow," Becky said. "I can't believe it. We are probably the first people inside here in years."

The beams of their flashlights followed the

ropes up to a crude wooden ceiling built of thick boards. The holes sawn in the ceiling were rough, but each had a hole with a rope through it. Twelve holes. Twelve ropes. One for each bell ringer.

And there were windows too. Actually, the windows were more like openings in the brick tower. The girls looked down and out on the sparkling town of Sleepy Hollow so quaint from a distance. No sign at all that the decorations were frightening instead of joyful. Even the grotesque Headless Horseman statue looked like another brave Civil War general. Just a peaceful, snowy village. Her parents and brothers were down there somewhere, watching TV, doing homework, cleaning up from supper— never knowing that someone that loved them was looking down on them at that moment.

"One of us has to get up there and check out the swing things," Honey said.

"I'll go," Claire said.

Honey took a breath and shook her head.

111

"No. I'm the leader."

"Do you want us to wait for you here?" Becky asked, slinging her flashlight beam in Honey's direction, but she only succeeded in awakening something vile. A black varmint swooped down toward them, darting between their heads with wicked precision before swinging around and speeding through them again on its way up.

The banister pressed into Honey's back as she tried to become one with the white paint on the walls. Claire was still ducking with her hands over her head, and Becky looked like she might faint.

"Was that a bat?" Becky gasped. "I can't believe I'm doing this."

Claire recovered quickly, caught one of the ropes and leaned her weight against it. "Shouldn't we give it try?"

"No!" Honey said. "If anyone hears them ringing, we're in trouble."

"Trouble, smouble. We succeeded. We proved that it isn't dangerous up here. We'll let the bells ring for Christmas Eve."

"Getting caught inside the church wasn't part of the deal," Becky said. "Let's go home and then next practice we can show Mrs. Keys . . ."

But Claire wasn't waiting. She grabbed onto one of the ropes and pulled—just a little at first. "Listen," she said. "Listen for the bell."

113

Nothing.

Silence.

Claire pulled harder.

But nothing.

"You did it too slow," Becky said. "You have to get the bell swinging faster."

"I'll try another one," Claire said. She walked over to the next rope, but Honey wasn't interested. Already a dread fear was filling her heart. Something wasn't right. Something was hidden. A plain wooden ladder made of ancient planks was nailed into the wall. It went up until it dead-ended at a trap door. She tucked her flashlight under her chin like she had seen her father do. She began climbing the ladder as fast as she could. She had to see the bells for herself. At the top, she put her head against the trapdoor and strained upward. It gave an inch at a time, raining dust and debris with every move. Finally it reached the tipping point and crashed open, clearing the way.

Honey climbed up the last rungs and studied the belfry in the moonlight.

It was empty.

No bells. Just the huge structures of wood beams and wheels. The twelve bronze bells were missing.

"THEY'RE GONE!" Honey called down to Becky and Claire. "The bells are gone."

"Impossible! Maybe they are farther up,"

114

Becky said.

"There isn't any more up!" Honey shouted. "Someone has stolen the bells."

No bells. No ringing. Nothing. She wouldn't ever hear them pealing across the hills and valleys like her mom remembered. Honey felt empty. The disappointment was more than missing out on something cool. It was almost like she missed seeing someone. Like being invited to a birthday party, but the birthday kid doesn't show up. That's what it felt like. An awful practical joke.

Honey climbed back down the ladder. "I can't believe it!"

Becky took her hand. "I'm sorry, Honey. I know you were counting on ringing them for the Christmas Eve service."

Claire dusted her hands. "I didn't expect this, but at least we have the Festival. It's going to be great."

Just great.

Honey looked around the room one last time because she still couldn't believe her eyes. How had they just disappeared? Bells that big, that heavy, couldn't be carried out in secret. Someone had to know something.

"We'd better go," Claire said. "Sarah will get suspicious if we wait too long."

But Honey was suspicious of something else. A deeper mystery. The mystery of the bells and why they were missing. She had to get to the bottom of this.

"I'm calling the reverend." Honey led the way down the stairs, no longer afraid of some spider webs and bats. They'd better be afraid of her because she was on a mission. They gathered their bags, exited through the self-locking doors, and by the time they were in Sarah's truck, Honey was scrolling for the phone number to the Cape Sanctuary Bed & Breakfast.

Becky nudged Honey's shoulder and gestured toward Sarah. They hadn't told Sarah the truth about the bells.

Honey sucked all the air out of the truck cabin and said, "Look, Sarah. We did something after practice, but you have to promise not to tell a single living soul."

Sarah pulled the truck along a curb on Mt. Sinai Road. "What? What did you girls do?"

Honey swallowed and then told her the whole story.

117

"So you see," Honey said, "we just wanted to ring the bells for Christmas to remind Sleepy Hollow that every day doesn't have to be Halloween."

Sarah shook her head. "You could have been killed."

"But we weren't," Becky said.

Honey tapped her phone. "I'm calling Reverend McAdams right now."

Sarah shook her head. "Great. Now I'm an accessory to your crimes."

"It's Honey again," Honey said into her phone. "Yeah, sorry to bother you, but since you were so worried about the belfry being dangerous, I thought you'd like to know that the stairs are fine, because me, Becky, and Claire went up them after practice. Mrs. Keys doesn't know. Please don't tell her, because we waited until she was gone. Anyway, the reason I'm calling is because I went up there to see if we could ring the bells, but the bells are gone!" Honey needed another deep breath before she could continue.

"Hello? Are you there?" Honey asked. "I couldn't hear you, but the bells are gone. There aren't any bells up there. We tried ringing them and nothing happened, so I went higher, and it's empty. The bells are nowhere. Did you know that? Do you know what happened to them?"

Here Honey waited while he sputtered. Reverend McAdams said something about forgetting and then something else about it happening before he came to Sleepy Hollow. He didn't remember exactly, but it seemed like he heard that the city had something to do with the remodeling of the steeple. They'd helped the church out. The selectmen would know.

"What's going on?" Sarah whispered. "Are you in trouble?"

Claire propped her feet on the dash of Sarah's truck. "The church is in trouble. If someone can carry those bells out of the church without them knowing, next thing you know, they'll be missing their pipe organ."

119

"Someone knows where they went," Honey said to the reverend, "and we're going to help you find them. Alright, then. Good night and sorry to call you again. See you on Christmas Eve."

She clicked off her phone.

"What did he say?" Sarah asked. Sarah might be Claire's big sister, but Honey still liked her. Not as much as Harry did, but that was a different story. "Did the city take them?"

"Something like that," Honey said. "Maybe we should talk to the selectmen—"

"I'll tell you this," said Sarah. "You won't learn anything by talking to the mayor or the selectmen. They have more secrets than Miss Fortissimo's diary. Harry says some of what the selectmen know is pretty dark. You need to do your own investigation. Find out when the North Church was remodeled or if there was repair work done. See who was in charge then. Do your homework." Sarah was on the school paper at the high school. She was the one who discovered the shrinking pudding portions in the cafeteria's lunches and started a petition. She was legit.

And Honey knew exactly where to go to dig up dirt.

The library.

MELTED

The last day of school before the winter break had been filled with practice and planning for the ultimate adventure—the Haunted Holiday Festival. With every description of the costumes, pranks, and frights, Honey's mood got darker and darker. Without the bells, they might as well cancel the play. Without the play, Honey would have to spend Christmas Eve in the new pit of despair constructed by the city of Sleepy Hollow, her dreams of a normal Christmas fading like a poinsettia in January.

Tonight, the girls only had an hour before practice started, so they had to hurry. They ran to the library as soon as school ended. Clomping in their snow boots through the gritty sidewalks, they splashed and laughed along the way. They were honing in. They could smell blood. Soon they'd find the culprit.

Honey was first to Maisie O'Brien, the librarian. Honey always thought she was a bit of an odd ball in Sleepy Hollow but also one of the most interesting. Miss O'Brien was not one to participate in all the Halloween stuff. And although she preferred to stay away, she always knew what was happening in town. She wore long, colorful skirts and scarves and perfectly round glasses that seemed to always dangle from her long nose. Miss O'Brien's red hair was wild and free and jutted out in all directions. But as strange as all that was for

Sleepy Hollow, Honey liked her and tried to find time to speak with her as much as possible. After all, they did both enjoy books and stories and looking things up—not on the computer but deep in the library archives and old dusty shelves where no one else went.

"Why, Honey Moon, as I live and breathe," Miss O'Brien said. "I've been expecting you."

Honey felt her brow wrinkle. "You were? But why?"

123

"Oh, dear me," the librarian said, "there's always a little shift in the wind when Honey Moon is near." Then she smiled, which gave Honey a peaceful feeling.

Becky and Claire leaned their tummies against the circulation desk. Miss O'Brien peered over the rims of her glasses at them.

"So you've brought your wee friends as well," Miss O'Brien said. "How can I be helpin' you?"

"We're looking for some Sleepy Hollow

history," Honey said. "Trying to learn something about our town."

Miss O'Brien leaned back with a smile. "Oh, good. I was afraid you wanted Christmas werewolf books. If I never see another frightful Christmas book, it would be too soon." She walked from behind the counter, and they followed her to the oldest part of the library, said to have been built a hundred years ago. "Do you know the dates you're looking for? We've had some problems with our old newspapers. Seems like they were printed with bad ink. It keeps disappearing, like someone doesn't want anyone to remember what's happened here."

Miss O'Brien looked directly at Honey and winked. "But with you and your brother on the case, perhaps we'll be getting to the bottom of it all one day."

Honey nodded.

"We don't know the exact date," Honey said, "but we want to know what happened to the church bells."

Miss O'Brien removed her glasses and folded her hands over her heart. "The church bells? That's a good question." She paused and a dreamy look came over her. "Now there's a mystery if ever there was one."

Honey cleared her throat.

Miss O'Brien walked toward a long table pushed against a back wall. "From my understandin', the bells last tolled just before Sleepy Hollow officially became what it is today. Sad to see all of our holidays disappear into one looooong Halloween." She went to a shelf of narrow slots and ran her finger down the stack. "Here we go. This is about the time they did the remodel on the North Church."

She passed her palm over the box, and Honey thought she saw the dust particles sparkle like tiny diamonds. Honey smiled. Becky sneezed. Claire looked bored.

"Can I trust you girls?" Miss O'Brien asked. "These papers are old and rare as dragon's teeth."

Honey nodded. "I do research in here all the time. I'll be careful."

The librarian fixed Claire with a skeptical eye. "A little birdie told me that one wee lass broke a window at that very church yer wonderin' about. Wouldn't want that kind of accident here."

Claire turned the brim of her baseball cap backwards and looked about as guilty as any girl could appear. There was just something about Miss O'Brien that made it hard to fib.

"As for you, Honey Moon," Miss O'Brien said, "seek the truth and you will find it."

Then Miss O'Brien turned with a flourish. She raised her right arm with a small wave. "I'll be in the front if you need me. Be careful, lasses, especially you, Honey Moon."

Honey closed her eyes for a moment and took a breath. She turned the old newspaper pages.

"See anything?" Claire asked.

"Hold your horses," Honey said. She scanned the first page and found nothing about the church. Scanning was easy because, just as Miss O'Brien said, there were whole sections of the paper that had faded. No words. Honey dearly hoped that somewhere those records existed. If someone could change history, they could change the future. Quickly she made it through the first few editions of the paper. Then on the fifth page of a February issue, she saw something, a blurry headline. Honey passed her palm over the paper, just as the librarian did. Honey raised one eyebrow as the headline sparkled into focus.

"Church remodel underway," she read aloud. "Kligore Construction has been hired to repair the worn and dangerous staircase of the North Church bell tower."

"It didn't look repaired to me," said Claire. "That staircase was ancient."

"Does it say anything about them removing the bells?" asked Becky.

Honey scanned. "Yes. It says the floor of the ringing chamber will be replaced and the staircases reinforced with new timber. Oh, and the bells will be removed, then returned after everything has been replaced."

"But nothing was fixed," said Claire. "They took the bells and didn't fix anything."

The rest of the article had faded into oblivion. Honey turned the page, wondering at all the important information that had been lost, or hidden. Surely there was a clue somewhere.

"So that's when it went up?" Becky pointed at a picture of the famous Headless Horseman statue on the square. The black-and-white photo was grainy, but the image was unmistakable. Atop the granite pedestal stood the bronze statue. It wasn't finished, but its grasping hands already held the sneering jack-o'-lantern. "I always wondered whose decision it was to build it."

"It says here that the selectmen voted to designate a spot on the town green to the statue, and the statue itself was donated by Kligore Construction." Honey kept her finger on the caption. "Donated by Kligore Construction? The bronze statue was donated by Kligore Construction? The same people who took the bells out of the church?"

"And didn't return them?" Claire's eyes blazed. "Of all the crummy, dirty tricks."

"I don't get it," said Becky. "Why?"

"Don't you see," Honey said. "They used the metal from the bells to make the Headless Horseman statue." Honey felt her knees shake. There were no bells left. The beautiful music had been destroyed for an ugly, hateful statue of a decapitated horseman. How had this stayed a secret? Didn't anyone care?

"Those selectmen, I'd like to ring their bells." Claire's anger was almost comforting.

Becky looked at her watch. "We have to hurry. We're going to be late to practice."

They gently boxed the old newspapers and headed back to Miss O'Brien.

"Did ya find what you needed?" Miss O'Brien asked.

"Yes," Honey said. "Kligore."

Miss O'Brien smiled as she adjusted a small framed picture on her desk. It was an image of a wild goose souring through dark clouds. "Of course it was."

"Well, I think he took the bells and used them to make that stupid statue."

"The Headless Horseman," Claire added.

"I know which statue she be speakin' of. That vile creature."

Honey looked at Miss O'Brien and caught a bright twinkle in her eye.

"So what now, Honey Moon?" Miss O'Brien asked.

"Gotta follow my leads and get to the bottom of it. And then I have to find a way to still make Christmas normal again."

"Ahhh, I have faith in ya, now. Just be careful as you tread."

Honey didn't look right or left but just stayed between Becky and Claire as they hurried to practice. The spooky colored lights from the storefronts lit their way until they turned down the darker streets of the neighborhoods and finally arrived at North Church.

131

But cars were pulling out of the parking lot.

"Did we miss practice?" Becky asked. "We're not late."

"There you are, girls," said Mrs. Keys. "I sent word to your parents, but you weren't home. We've canceled the Christmas Eve program. Reverend McAdams told me there was no chance of doing a bell ringing. And besides, the school choir is performing across the street at the Haunted Holiday Festival at the same time.

We've had too many kids drop out." She looked sad and disappointed. "Can't beat Halloween."

"I don't quit," Honey said. "I'll be a shepherd and angel both. I can learn the lines. The four of us will do the whole thing."

"Maybe next year," Mrs. Keys said. "This year, let's just go and enjoy the festival. It's what everyone wants to do, evidently."

132 Claire clapped a hand on Honey's back. "Sorry it didn't work out for you, but life ain't fair. Why don't you come to the festival with me? We can put together a gross costume for you. I've got it! Mrs. Claus the Vampire Slayer. That could be you."

Becky giggled. "C'mon, Honey. Say you'll do it. You'll get bonus points in choir."

"I don't know. I can't decide right now." Honey dug her toe in the snow. "I'll let you know tomorrow."

"Okay," Becky said. "Let's go home."

They walked around the park, past the twisted, winter wonderland. Lights shone and twinkled as the workers made the last-minute adjustments. Fires crackled in large metal drums with the name Kligore imprinted on them. Honey grimaced.

"Look at the gingerbread house," Becky cried. "When did that go up?"

The life-sized gingerbread house was covered in candy and icing with a white stone walkway lined with giant lollipops on either side. It didn't look scary at all. Honey felt a little better. A gingerbread house. That was fun, cheerful, and Christmassy. Maybe she could find something that didn't scream Halloween.

"It's real candy," Claire said. She poked at a gumdrop on the wall and motioned to a woman on a ladder who was gluing graham cracker shingles on the roof with icing. "Can I eat this?"

The woman's eyes gleamed. "Tomorrow you can. I'll be all ready for the little boys and girls tomorrow. Bring your friends."

"We can't wait!" Becky clapped her hands and then turned to Honey and said, "See, it's not all scary. See you tomorrow."

Honey started out on the long walk home. Discovering the bells had been melted down was the worst thing that had happened all year. She'd now have to try and make the best of the holiday. She still had her Christmas present to open on Christmas Eve. She'd finally have her gown and that was going to be splendiferous. Or so she thought.

FOR SUCH A TIME AS THIS

"I don't want to be Mrs. Claus, Vampire Slayer,"
Honey said over the phone. "Claire's crazy."
Dress up pretty, then," Becky suggested.
"Have you got your holiday dress, yet? You
could wear it and be the Star of Christmas."

Honey stopped chewing the end of her braid. Would she have time to get dressed up after they opened their gifts? She wrapped the braid around her finger, hoping for some curl. Maybe Mom would even let her wear lip gloss. And maybe Scooter would see her.

"Maybe Scooter will see you," Becky said, reading her mind like only a best friend can do.

"Gross!" Honey said. "That's disgusting." But she looked in the mirror all the same, wondering what the dress looked like and if it was warm enough to wear without her coat. "I'll call you if I decide to come," she said finally. "But I'm not singing in the school choir. Miss Fortissimo isn't getting her Christmas wish."

"Honey," her mother called. "Are you ready for presents?"

"Gotta go!" Honey hung up and skipped into the living room. The Moons always went full tilt on the decorations. They had a large Douglas fir tree decorated with natural and glass ornaments. Honey's favorite was the red glass heart. It was very delicate, paper-thin glass that allowed the twinkling lights on the tree to shine through. A large wreath made of pinecones with a huge green ribbon hung over the mantle. The nativity scene was on the oak mantle, minus one astronaut shepherd who was still in orbit. Pine roping stretched all around the room with tiny white lights wrapped around the evergreen garland. Honey paused a second to take it all in. But only for a second because it was hard not to throw herself under the tree and grab her gift.

She just needed to get the dress opened, and then she could see if it gave her the nerve to go to the Haunted Holiday Festival.

Everyone was already around the tree. Harvest was busy stacking and re-stacking the five packages, hoping to be the closest one when his dad, who was wearing a Santa hat, gave the order to unwrap.

"Finally," Harry said. "What've you been doing? Carving your and Scooter's initials in your closet door?"

131

"Guess who picked me up from practice this week," Honey said. "Sarah Sinclair. Don't believe she mentioned you at all."

That was all it took to shut Harry up. One mention of Sarah's name and he wouldn't be able to speak until New Year's Day.

"You two," said Mary. "Behave yourselves. It's time for presents."

The way her mom's eyes shone, Honey thought she must be really excited about what she was getting, but even after she opened her new purse, she still looked just as excited. Could it be that she was happier giving the presents away than getting one?

Honey's dad unwrapped a new gearshift knob for Emma, the MG-F convertible he was restoring.

"Just what I wanted," he said looking at Mary. "How did you know?"

"A little birdy told me," Mary said with a wink.

"More likely the catalog pages Dad left lying around the house," Harry said.

"Yeah, you even circled the knob with a red Sharpie, Dad. Come on," Honey added.

"So I'm not subtle," John Moon said.

Next, Mary Moon handed Harry a flat package in shiny silver paper.

"For me?" He tried to act cool, but he was as restless as Harvest. Harry removed the paper, opened the box, and stared at the wrapping inside. "It's from Bride of Frankenstein?"

Honey rose to her knees. Had her mom given him the wrong present? But her mom nodded. Something wasn't right. Harry lifted the plastic sleeve off the hanger and shook out a flash of red satin and velvet.

"It's a new cape!" he said. "This will be perfect for my magic show!"

Honey rubbed her eyes as Harry took it

off the hanger. The red satin was only the lining. Tied around his neck, the red velvet in the cape caught the light and looked like

something alive. How funny that they were both getting things from the same store.

Mary Moon presented Honey with the next gift wrapped in blue paper dotted with tiny green trees. Maybe she was getting a dressy costume for the stage as well. Perhaps she was going to be Harry's assistant. She bit her lip. He'd never let her on stage before, but with her matching red prom gown, it'd look perfect. She'd know exactly how to do everything. She'd even be better than Sarah.

The paper ripped, and the tape broke with a pop. Honey forced the box open, but instead of touching soft satin, she felt something lumpy. The bright colors looked more at home in a preschool than a formal clothing store. Then she saw the horrible head. Googly eyes caught hers. Every spot on the turtle shell was a different color, and the bald turtle head reflected the Christmas tree lights.

False alarm.

She closed the box and grimaced. "This isn't my present. This is for Harvest."

Her mother's smile hardened. "No, it's for you."

"Mom," Honey leaned forward. "It's the T-U-R-T-L-E. It's for Harvest."

Her dad turned to her mom with a questioning look.

"No, dear," Mary said. "What would Harvest need with a backpack? We noticed that your book bag is looking shabby. Time for a new one, and this one just spoke your name."

142

Honey stared at the turtle in silent horror. Unless her name was Nerdy Turtle Girl, there was a mistake. Then she darted a look at the fabulous cape Harry was flying around the room in. This could not possibly be happening.

"What is Harvest getting?" she asked.

"What's that have to do with it?" Mary asked.

Honey dropped the backpack. "I'll trade him. I don't care what it is, it can't be worse. Mom, I'm in fifth grade." Nothing about this Christmas was going right. Not one single thing. She stood to go, trying very hard not to cry.

"Honey," her dad said, "you will pick up your gift, take it to your room, and you will give your mom a hug before you leave. You might be disappointed, but your mom thought long and hard about that gift."

How could her mom think that Honey, her ten-year-old daughter, wanted a preschool turtle backpack? She would never carry it. Never. Honey stomped upstairs to her room. She slammed the door, threw the turtle against the wall, and flopped on her bed.

143

Worst.
Christmas.
Ever.

Why did she have to be the little sister of a celebrity who gets a splendiferous new cape? Why couldn't she have a normal Christmas and not a spooky one? Why did she have to live in Sleepy Hollow?

"Because that's where you are needed."

Honey lifted her head. Where had that voice

come from? Great! Now she was going crazy. Besides, no one needed her. If she wasn't here, Becky and Claire could be friends without her. Reverend McAdams wouldn't have to answer the phone when he was on vacation. Harvest could keep the disgusting turtle backpack, and Harry would go along being good and famous.

"We go where we are needed. You are here because you are needed."

Honey turned to the turtle, but it only looked back with those big googly eyes that seemed to see everything. Was it talking to her? No way. But Honey wouldn't let anyone or anything get the last word.

"I tried to bring the holiday back to Sleepy Hollow. I tried to remind everyone the reason for this season. It's not Halloween. Every day does not have to be Halloween night. I did everything I could. I even tried to get the bells to ring, but they were stolen and no one even cares. Everyone is busy with their own Halloween stuff. They won't listen to me because they think I am just a kid when I tell them that there could be something bigger. Something grander."

"Show them. Seek the truth."

She wasn't a magician. That was Harry's talent. All she had was a fighting personality and a strong sense of right versus wrong.

"Be there."

Even if she was upset? Even if she was the only one who wanted something different? Even if she was alone?

"You are never alone."

Honey looked at the ugly turtle again. It hadn't moved. Nothing had moved but everything had changed. This was the night the world celebrated the homecoming of its Master. The last night that darkness would rule unchallenged. This was not a night for her to hide. It was the time for light, and darkness only made the light shine brighter.

She would go to the Haunted Holiday Festival.

146

THEIR OLD, FAMILIAR CAROLS PLAY

"It's Christmas Eve," Honey whispered. "It's Christmas Eve. I'm here to have fun." She had brought her new, ugly turtle backpack with her—at least it would fit in. It was kind of a costume. And besides, Honey couldn't help but feel a little comforted with the thing on her back. Turtle was there, and she was not alone.

The vampire Santa statue stood at the main entrance beneath the banner that read, "Welcome to the Sleepy Hollow Haunted Holiday Festival." She kept her eyes down, not looking at his face and trying not to notice his blood-stained gloves.

"You are a NUMBSKULL!" she said as she passed the statue.

"ARRRGGGHHHH!"

Honey jumped and covered her eyes. Her heart had nearly stopped, but now it was racing. At the sound of laughter, she braved a peek. It was Scooter, dressed like an evil elf or a troll with warts and moles that had tufts of hair sticking out of an almost bald, pimply head.

"Scared you!" He laughed like a hyena.

Honey pulled herself up to her full height. She would not let Scooter and his stupid prank get the best of her. She assumed her warrior attitude.

"I helped you with your paper. Why are you being mean?"

"Because it's the Haunted Holiday Festival," Scooter said. "It's what you're supposed to do. Scare people. And hey, that stupid backpack sure is scary."

149

"It's Christmas Eve," she said. "You don't scare people on Christmas Eve. And just don't worry about my backpack—it's special."

"Ooooo sorry, Your Highness. But maybe your next essay should be about Sleepy Hollow and why we like to scare people."

Honey waved him away. She was over him. So over him. "Leave me alone," she said. He wasn't cute anymore. And he didn't even write good essays.

Honey wandered into the green and walked among the tents with shoulders hunched.

Everyone wore Halloween costumes, most with a red ribbon or tinsel added for some lame Christmas effect, but they were still grotesque. Here and there she saw kids from her class, but the choir wasn't singing yet. She didn't recognize most of the people. She assumed they were strangers. Probably tourists wanting to get scared on Christmas. Well, they sure came to the right place.

A huge Christmas tree decorated with spiders, bats, and bones stood in front of the Clock Tower. A punch bowl flickered with weird lights, and strange smoke poured out of it. Honey stood by the cookie table. The sugar cookies looked good, but on closer inspection the angels looked more like something from Doctor Who than the nativity. Then she saw Isabela standing near the tree.

Isabela was in costume. She was dressed like a doctor, well, a veterinarian. Isabela was animal crazy and wanted to work with animals when she got older. Maybe as a vet or maybe even a marine biologist.

Isabela picked up a cookie. "Hi, Honey. How come you're not wearing a costume?"

Honey shrugged. "Don't want to. I can't stand that they took Christmas away from us."

"Who did?" Isabela bit into the cookie. "Uhm. Pretty good."

151

"The mayor. All this kooky Halloween haunted stuff. We couldn't have our pageant because of it."

"Oooo," Isabela said. "That stinks. But I guess you can't do anything. Like my mom says, you can't beat city hall."

Honey smiled. Not because of what Isabela said but because Isabela was pretty new to town. She had been a foster child and was recently adopted by a nice couple in Sleepy Hollow. A couple with a huge Saint Bernard, which suited Isabela just fine.

"I guess I can't really fight city hall, but I need to do something. Even if I can't bring the bells back."

Isabel gave Honey a funny look. "Bells?"

"Oh, it's a long story. But there used to be bells in the church tower. I wanted to ring them tonight."

Just then, Honey saw a black car whiz past the green down Main Street. It had an odd golden hood ornament that had been broken. It happened on Halloween when Harry Moon stopped Mayor Kligore from pulling off one of his horrible, scary Halloween deeds.

On the license plate were the words We Drive By Night. She shivered but not because of the cold. Then she saw Miss O'Brien standing near the Clock Tower. Honey waved. Miss O'Brien waved, and then she was gone—hidden in the shadows. But still, just seeing the librarian made Honey shiver again—but this time is was a deep shiver, the kind you get when something truly wonderful or miraculous happens.

Honey walked among the different vendors, games, and societies sponsoring the party and looked for any sign of truth.

The music blared. There were screams of laughter as people were startled. *Nothing wrong with having fun,* Honey told herself. And yet, something was missing. Something was being deliberately suppressed, and it took a lot of darkness to hide it. No amount of special effects could cover the void.

153

She came at last to the gingerbread house, and that's where she found Becky and Claire. Honey couldn't stop looking at Claire's awful dripping-snowman outfit. And she couldn't help but notice the edible bones now being offered from the once-innocent gingerbread house. Claire and Becky broke off skeleton pieces and nibbled like mice.

"Hey, guys," Honey said.

"This is so good." Claire didn't even look at her. She broke off a chunk of clavicle.

"Mmm, the best candy in the world," Becky agreed. Becky had a licorice stick in one hand and a handful of Skittles in the other. At least her pony costume wasn't scary.

"You don't even like licorice," Honey said.

"This is different." Becky crammed the licorice in her mouth and pulled another strip off the fake shutters. Her hoof mittens were getting sticky.

"Here, have some." Claire plucked a cone of cotton-candy off a bush that was planted beneath the window.

It had to be sweet to cover what was missing.

"No, thanks," Honey said. "I guess you noticed I'm not wearing a beautiful yellow satin gown. Just this ugly turtle."

But they hadn't. They were having fun without her.

Pointy-toed boots emerged from the doorway. Honey recognized the woman who'd been decorating earlier that week, only this time she was dressed as a witch with a piece of mistletoe stuck in her black hat. "Yes, have some candy," she said. "Or you can come inside when you're ready. I think your friends are about ready."

The way her eyes looked them over gave Honey chills. She couldn't remember a witch at a Christmas gingerbread house. She stepped back and looked at the house again. This wasn't a winter story. It was Hansel and Gretel, and her friends were eating like pigs.

155

"Let's go," she said. Didn't Becky and Claire know how Hansel and Gretel ended? She had to get them out of there. "Don't you have to sing in the school choir?"

Claire shrugged. "Not worried about it."

"Come on," Honey said. "With your voice, you probably need the extra credit to pass the class."

Becky chewed on the licorice. "We don't have to sing for another hour. We have a lot of time."

An hour? Honey looked around her. People bumping into each other, shoving at a game to get first pick over the prizes. The emcee was announcing the winners of the scariest nutcracker award. She couldn't last another hour. Becky and Claire didn't seem to feel the same darkness she felt. They didn't understand. With the Christmas play now canceled, Honey had no choice but to stay and sing with the school choir. She couldn't face this alone. A child cried as a mean dog on a leash barked. People booed at the unpopular choice of winner at the nutcracker contest. All the noise, the clamor, all of this going on instead of a silent, peaceful night. All she wanted was a normal Christmas, something people expected. Not this.

She had to find a way to remind everyone, the whole town, that Christmas cannot be hidden behind some creepy statues and paint and spider webs. If only the bells could ring out.

She looked toward North Church and remembered something Reverend McAdams had said. "Get some jingle bells."

Jingle bells. Honey felt Turtle grow a little heavier on her back. She let the backpack slip off her shoulders. For the first time since she got the thing, she unzipped its neon-green shell. Inside she found some small silver jingle bells attached to a long red ribbon. Twelve bells.

"How? Why?" Honey rooted around in the bag and found a card—a regular, old Christmas card with no Santa skeletons on it or spiders or skulls. Just a pretty, normal, regular Christmas tree. Honey opened the card.

Wishing you
the merriest
and brightest
Christmas.

But also, written below that, there was some handwriting.

I THOUGHT THESE MIGHT
COME IN HANDY,
LOVE
HARRY, YOUR BIG BROTHER

158   Honey needed to swipe a few tears from her eyes. Harry knew. Harry always knew. She looked toward the church again. She couldn't risk climbing the tower. Not now. She glanced around the green. The Clock Tower.

    With Turtle bouncing on her back Honey ran to the tower. She climbed the steps to the top. "I go where I am needed." She looked out at the teeming crowd. Loud rock music blared from the speakers. Voices and laughter and even a few baby cries swam through the air. Honey looked at her small ribbon of bells. No way could these bells drown those sounds. No one would hear.

"Come on, Turtle," Honey said, defeated. "Let's go home."

But before she could take a step, she spotted Miss O'Brien near an old oak tree. Miss O'Brien waved her hand in the air, and in that instant, there was crackle in the air and all the music was silenced. Now all Honey could hear were the groans and complaints of the festival goers.

"Up here!" she called.

159

Honey jingled the bells as hard as she could. Their sound seemed to grow and multiply as they rang out over the green. A sound that seemed to soar and wrap itself around all the people and all the dreadful displays.

This was the sound of Christmas itself; an ancient sound that'd pealed for two thousand years. That was the song filling the emptiness. As she jingled the ribbon, she saw Mrs. Keys climb onto the makeshift stage where the band played. She sat down at the piano and began to play.

Slowly, Mrs. Keys began to sing. Her voice grew stronger and stronger and clearer.

And in despair I bowed my head.
"There is no peace on earth," I said,
"For hate is strong and mocks the song
Of peace on earth, goodwill to men!"

Then pealed the bells more loud and deep:
"God is not dead, nor doth He sleep!
The Wrong shall fail, the Right prevail
With peace on earth, goodwill to men."

Again, Honey swiped tears from her eyes. Christmas had found its way to Sleepy Hollow.

The music faded. Calm settled on the crowd like a warm blanket. A hoot owl could be heard back at the town square. And was that a cow mooing from Folly Farm?

Honey tucked the bells into the backpack and skittered down the Clock Tower steps. The rock band played again and folks went back to their haunted festival. Honey walked through the crowd in search of Mrs. Keys.

"That was unbelievable." It was Mrs. Keys catching up with Honey. "We might not have had our pageant, Honey Moon, but that was quite a performance. Thank you."

"You too," Honey said, but her voice was drowned out by the crowd. Becky, Claire, and Isabela joined them.

"You did it, Honey Moon," Becky said. "You rang the bells."

A man with a hideous furry face, scratching at the hair glued on his cheek, approached Honey. "The boss ain't gonna like this. He hates bells." He squinted his bloodshot eyes at Honey. "Hey, you're that magic kid's sister."

Honey pulled herself up to her full height. "I sure am."

The man scratched his face again. "Just wait. I'm sure the boss will take care of you and those bells. He hates bells, reminds him of . . . well, of Christmas past. That's why we removed—" He stopped talking. But Honey had heard enough.

"You'll see," the dog-man said. "Boss will make an ordinance against bells of any kind. You'll see." He trotted off toward Folly Farm

Honey could only smile. No ordinance on paper could stand against the power that'd quaked the earth that night. An arrival. A reclaiming, like the trumpet blast when a king takes his throne. For one night, Halloween had met its match.

162

All this time, Honey had been longing for a normal Christmas—Santa, carols, trees with lights and tinsel. Now she understood that those traditions were fun, but they weren't strong enough to hold back the darkness. It wasn't a normal Christmas that would fill the hole in Sleepy Hollow. It was something stronger than that. It was in the heart of every man or woman and boy or girl who loved what was good and right. That's what would eventually win the fight against Halloween.

I go where I am needed.

Honey Moon shrugged Turtle off her shoulders. She held him at arm's length and peered into his googly eyes. "Looks like it's you and me. Together always. Merry Christmas, Turtle."

164

Honey Moon's Normal Christmas Cookbook

Hi Girlfriend,

Thanks for coming along on my Christmas adventure. I've got to say, I'm kind of glad it's over but even more glad that I got to hear the bells on Christmas Eve. Just between you and me, I was a little scared those steps in the bell tower might crash.

But what Christmas is complete without some cookies and fun craft ideas?

I've been hanging out in my room with Becky and Claire, and we came up with some truly splendiferous goodies and crafts that are easy to bake and easy to make.

My favorite is the Peanut Butter Bells. Especially when they are still warm, just out of the oven, and the chocolate is all soft and melty. Uhmm, I can taste them now.

So, go ahead and turn the pages to find some ideas to brighten your holidays even more.

And thanks again for coming along, and be sure to visit me on the web where you can share your ideas with me. How cool is that?

Love,

Honey

167

P.S. Remember: Always assemble all your ingredients, bowls, and measuring spoons and cups before starting any recipe. There's a technical term for this. It's *mise en place*—that's a French culinary term that means set in place.

Oh, and if you need help in the kitchen, be sure to ask.

PEANUT BUTTER BELLS

You might want to make extra. These go fast. And be careful, your brother or your sister might even hug you.

Ingredients:

1/2	cup granulated sugar
1	cup packed brown sugar
1	cup creamy peanut butter
1	cup butter or margarine, softened
2	eggs
3	cups all-purpose flour
1 1/2	teaspoons baking soda
1	teaspoon baking powder

About 7 dozen chocolate bells. (You can usually find them in the bulk candy section of the grocery store.)

Additional granulated sugar (about 2 tablespoons)

Directions:

- Heat oven to 375°F. In a large bowl, beat the 1/2 cup granulated sugar, the brown sugar, peanut butter, butter, and eggs with an electric mixer on medium speed, or mix with a big spoon. Stir in the flour,

168

baking soda, and baking powder.

- Shape dough into 1-inch balls; roll in the additional granulated sugar. Place about 2 inches apart on ungreased cookie sheet.

- Bake 8 to 10 minutes or until edges are light brown. Immediately press 1 chocolate bell in the center of each cookie. Remove from cookie sheet and place on a wire rack.

And try to save some for family and guests! They are scrumptious.

169

SUGAR BELLS

Now these are pretty easy. You can make your own cookie dough from scratch or use store bought; the kind in the tube is fine.

Don't forget: *Mise en place*

From Scratch

Ingredients:

Cookies

1 1/2 cups powdered sugar

1   cup butter or margarine, softened

1   teaspoon vanilla

1/2   teaspoon almond extract (optional)

1   egg

2 1/2 cups all-purpose flour

1   teaspoon baking soda

1   teaspoon cream of tartar

Plenty of candy sprinkles, nonpareils, or colored sugars for decorating.

Icing:

2   cups powdered sugar

1/2   teaspoon vanilla

2   tablespoons milk or half-and-half

Directions:

- In a large bowl, mix 1 1/2 cups powdered sugar, butter, 1 teaspoon vanilla, almond extract, and egg until well blended. Stir in flour, baking soda, and cream of tartar. <u>Cover and refrigerate at least 3 hours</u>. Now you can take a break and go read a book or go outside and play.

- Heat oven to 375°F. Divide dough in half. On a lightly floured, cloth-covered surface, roll out each half of the dough to 3/16 of an inch (or so—doesn't have to be exact). Cut into bell shapes with your cookie cutter. Oh, I almost forgot, if cookies are to be hung as decorations, make a hole in each 1/4 inch from the top with the end of a plastic straw. Place on ungreased cookie sheet.

- Bake 7 to 8 minutes or until light brown. Remove from cookie sheet and place on a cooling rack. Cool completely, about 30 minutes.

- In medium bowl, beat all frosting ingredients until smooth and spreadable. Tint with food color if desired. Frost and decorate cookies as desired with frosting and colored sugars.

171

Sugar Bells (Not from Scratch)

These are easy and quick and good to use if you ever have a cookie emergency. Hey, it could happen.

Open up the tube of the cookie dough. Break the log in half and then roll out on a floured surface.

Easy peasy, right?

Then just cut out your bells. Bake according to the package directions and decorate with colored sugars or icing.

Here's a recipe that my mother told me has been in our family for years and years.

GINGERBREAD COOKIES

This is a great recipe for making gingerbread boys or girls. Or you can even use it to make a gingerbread house or maybe you can try and build the North Church bell tower. Wow!

This recipe is the best. And it makes your house smell good too—mmmmm.

172

Ingredients:

1	cup packed brown sugar
1/3	cup shortening
1 1/2	cups dark molasses (It's sooooo sticky. Don't get it in your hair.)
2/3	cup cold water
7	cups all-purpose flour
2	teaspoons baking soda
2	teaspoons ground ginger
1	teaspoon ground allspice
1	teaspoon ground cloves
1	teaspoon ground cinnamon
1/2	teaspoon salt

I like to decorate my gingerbread boys and girls with raisin eyes and buttons and royal icing.

Directions:

- Mix brown sugar, shortening, molasses, and water in large bowl. Stir in flour, baking soda, ginger, allspice, cloves, cinnamon, and salt. Cover and refrigerate about 2 hours or until firm.

- Heat oven to 350°F. Grease cookie sheet lightly. Roll 1/4 of the dough at a time to 1/4-inch thickness on a floured surface. Cut with a floured gingerbread cookie cutter or other favorite shaped cutter. I like to make gingerbread reindeer. Place cookies about 2 inches apart on cookie sheet. Add raisins for eyes and buttons.

- Bake 10 to 12 minutes or until almost no indentation remains when touched in center. Immediately remove from cookie sheet. Cool on wire rack.

Frost cookies with royal icing and decorate however you want.

Royal Icing

1   1-pound box of 10X sugar
1   teaspoon cream of tartar
3   egg whites

Put in a mixing bowl and use an electric mixer to beat ingredients until thick and shiny. This takes about 5 minutes. Put icing in a resealable freezer bag and nip off one corner so you can pipe the icing out. Don't nip off too much or the icing will ooze out all over the place. This icing dries very quickly, so any you don't use should be stored in a plastic airtight container. It dries quickly and hard, so it's good for "gluing" cookies together and putting on candy decorations.

1/4

Blockhead Brownies

This is an easy recipe for fudgy brownies. After they bake, cut them into large squares, about two-inches all around. Then use royal icing to draw funny faces on them. Fun!

Ingredients:
1/2   cup vegetable oil

1   cup sugar
1   teaspoon vanilla
2   large eggs
1/4   teaspoon baking powder
1/3   cup cocoa powder
1/4   teaspoon salt
1/2   cup all-purpose flour

Preheat oven to 350°.
Mix oil and sugar until well blended.
Add eggs and vanilla; stir just until blended.
Mix all dry ingredients in a separate bowl.
Stir dry ingredients into the oil/sugar mixture.
Pour into greased 9 x 9 square pan.
Bake for 20 minutes or until sides just start
     to pull away from the pan.
Cool completely before cutting.

175

  Honey Note:
  This recipe can be doubled very easily. Just
double the ingredients and bake in a 9 x 13 pan.
If you double the recipe, you will need to cook
longer than 20 minutes.

SOFI BENITEZ

Author Sofi Benitez loves telling stories of living in bravery and enjoying a joyful life. She believes everyone has an important story to tell, and Sofi's motto, Be Brave, has become an empowering saying for Honey Moon and her friends. Sofi's favorite things are playing with her dog, Romeo, singing, and helping friends and strangers in need. The rest of the time, Sofi spends creating enchanting adventures for young girls encouraging them to grasp their power, live heroically, and sparkle away.

MARK ANDREW POE

Honey Moon creator Mark Andrew Poe never thought about creating a town where kids battled right and wrong. His dream was to love and care for animals, specifically his friends in the rabbit community.

Along the way, Mark became successful in all sorts of interesting careers. He entered the print and publishing world as a young man, and his company did really, really well. Mark also became a popular and nationally sought-after health care advocate for the care and well-being of rabbits.

Years ago, Mark came up with the idea of a story about a young boy with a special connection to a world of magic, all revealed through a remarkable rabbit friend.

Mark worked on his idea for several years before building a collaborative creative team to help him bring his idea to life.

Harry Moon was born. The team was thrilled when Mark introduced Harry's enchanting sister, Honey Moon. Boy, did she pack an unexpected punch!

In 2014, Mark began a multi-book project to launch Harry Moon and Honey Moon into the youth marketplace. Harry and Honey are kids who understand the difference between right and wrong. Kids who tangle with magic and forces unseen in a town where "every day is Halloween night." Today, Mark and the creative team continue to work on the many stories of Harry and Honey and the characters of Sleepy Hollow. He lives in suburban Chicago with his wife and his twenty-five rabbits.

BE SURE TO READ THE
CONTINUING AND ENCHANTED
ADVENTURES OF HONEY MOON.

Honey Moon's
DNA

Builds friendships that matter
Goes where she is needed
Helps fellow classmates
Speaks her mind
Honors her body
Does not categorize others
Loves to have a blast
Seeks wisdom from adults
Desires to be brave
Sparkles away
And, of course, loves her mom

COMING SOON!
MORE MAGICAL ADVENTURES

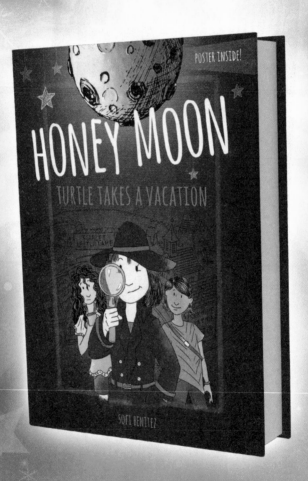

HONEY MOON

TURTLE TAKES A VACATION

POSTER INSIDE!

SOFI BENITEZ

HARRY MOON'S
DNA

Helps his fellow schoolmates
Makes friends with those who had once been his enemies
Respects nature
Honors his body
Does not categorize people too quickly
Seeks wisdom from adults
Guides the young
Controls his passions
Is curious
Understands that life will have trouble and accepts it
And, of course, loves his mom!

FOR MORE BOOKS
& RESOURCES GO TO
HARRYMOON.COM